Bᴇɴɴᴏ Tᴀ... tion, his t... head swimming with fatigue. He saw his stomach open, the bare organs—slick and wet in their own pulsing blood—staring up nakedly at him. A grizzled little man, with sharp spikes of white beard dotting his cheeks, was carefully settling a knobbed and calibrated block of metal into the flesh. He caught a glimpse of the operating lamp's idiot glare above him, and promptly fainted again.

When he awoke the second time, he was in a cold, cold room, lying naked to the groin on an operating table, his head slightly higher than his feet. The red, puckered scar that ran from the bottom of his rib cage to the inside of his thigh stared up at him. It reminded him of a crimson river coursing through desert land. The pin-head gleam of a metal wire-tip stuck up in the center of the scar. Abruptly, he remembered.

They stopped his screaming by forcing a wadded towel in his mouth.

**—from Harlan Ellison's *Run for the Stars***

Other Tor SF Doubles you may enjoy

*A Meeting with Medusa* by Arthur C. Clarke
b/w *Green Mars* by Kim Stanley Robinson

*The Ugly Little Boy* by Isaac Asimov
b/w *The [Widget], the [Wadget], and Boff* by
Theodore Sturgeon

*Houston, Houston, Do You Read?* by James
Tiptree, Jr.
b/w *Souls* by Joanna Russ

*The Saturn Game* by Poul Anderson
b/w *Iceborn* by Gregory Benford & Paul A. Carter

*Ill Met in Lankhmar* by Fritz Leiber
b/w *The Fair in Emain Macha* by Charles de Lint

*The Pugnacious Peacemaker* by Harry Turtledove
b/w *The Wheels of If* by L. Sprague de Camp

*Fugue State* by John M. Ford
b/w *The Death of Doctor Island* by Gene Wolfe

*Eye for Eye* by Orson Scott Card
b/w *The Tunesmith* by Lloyd Biggle, Jr.

# Harlan ELLISON
# RUN FOR THE STARS

# Jack DANN & Jack C. HALDEMAN II
# ECHOES OF THUNDER

TOR

A TOM DOHERTY ASSOCIATES BOOK
NEW YORK

Tor SF Double No. 32

RUN FOR THE STARS

This publication represents the first correct, author-emended text of *Run for the Stars* since its original magazine appearance in 1957. *This* is the preferred text.

ECHOES OF THUNDER

A Tor Book
Published by Tom Doherty Associates, Inc.
49 West 24th Street
New York, N.Y. 10010

Cover art by Barclay Shaw

ISBN: 0-812-51180-8

First edition: April 1991

Printed in the United States of America

0  9  8  7  6  5  4  3  2  1

# Run for the Stars

# I

THEY FOUND HIM LOOTING WHAT WAS LEFT OF
the body of a fat shopkeeper. He was hun-
kered down with his back to the blasted
storefront, picking through the hundred-
pockets of the dead merchant's work-bib.

He didn't hear them come in. The scream
of the Kyban ships scorching the city's
streets mingled too loudly with the screams
of the dying.

They crept up behind him, three men with
grimy faces and determined stares. The
roar of a power terminal exploding somewhere across the city covered the crackle
of their boots in the powdered and pebbled
concrete that littered the floor. They
stopped, and a man with blond hair nodded

to the other two. They grabbed him suddenly, twisting his hands up behind his back, bringing a sharp, surprised scream from him.

Bills and change tinkled from his hands, scattered across the rubble-strewn floor.

Benno Tallant twisted his head painfully and looked up at the men holding him. "Lemme go! He was dead! I only wanted to get enough money to buy food with! Honest to God, lemme go!" Tears gathered in the corners of his eyes from the pains in his twisted arms.

One of the men holding him—a stocky, plump man of indeterminate age and a lisping speech—snapped, "In case you hadn't noticed, lootie, this is a grocery you were robbing. There's food all over the shop. Why not use that?"

He gave the arm he held another half-twist.

Tallant bit his lip. There was no use arguing with these men; he couldn't tell them the money was to get narcotics. They would kill him and that would be the end of it. This was a time of war, the city was under siege from the Kyben, and they killed looters. Perhaps it was better that way; in death the insatiable craving for the dream-dust would stop, and he would be free. Even dead he would be free.

Free, to walk without the aid of the dream-dust; free, to lead a normal life. Yes, that was what he wanted, to be free . . . he would never touch the dream-dust again, if he came out of this alive.

And the pusher was probably dead, anyhow.

The thought of death—as it usually did—sent chills coursing down through his legs, numbing his muscles. He sagged in their grip.

The pig-faced man, who had not spoken, grunted in disgust. "This the best we can do, for Christ's sake? There's *got* to be someone in the group better for this job. Look at the miserable little slob, he's practically jelly."

The blond man shook his head. He was obviously the leader of the group. A patch of high forehead was miraculously clean among the filth and grime of his skin; he rubbed his hand over his forehead now, blotting away the clean area. "No, Shep, I think this is our man."

He turned to Tallant, stooped down and studied the quaking looter. He put his hand to Tallant's right eye, and spread the lids. "A junkie. Perfect." He stood up, added, "We've been looking for you all day, fellow."

"I never saw you before in my life, what do you want with me? Lemme go, willya!" They were taking too long to kill him—something was wrong.

His voice was rising in pitch, almost hys-

5

terically. Sweat poured down over his face as though a stream had been opened at the hairline.

The tall, blond man spoke hurriedly, glancing over his shoulder. "Come on, let's get him out of here. We'll let Doc Budder go to work on him." He motioned them to lift the quaking man, and as he rose, added, "There's a good five hours' work there," and he patted Tallant's lean stomach.

The lisping man named Shep said, "And those yellow bastards up there may not give us that long."

The pig-faced man nodded agreement, and as though to punctuate their feelings, a woman's high-pitched scream struck through the fast-falling dusk. They stopped, and Tallant thought he might go mad, right there, right in their arms, because of the scream, and these men, and no dust, and the entire world shattering around him. He wanted very badly to lie down and shiver.

He tried to slump again, but the pig-faced man dragged him erect.

They made their way through the shop, kicking up fine clouds of concrete dust and stepping on bits of plasteel that crackled beneath their feet. They paused at the shambles of the storefront, and peered into the gathering darkness.

"It's going to be a rough four miles back," the lisping man said; and the tall, blond leader silently nodded agreement.

6

Outside, the explosion of a fuel reservoir superimposed itself over the constant blast and scream of Kyban attack ... and the mere scream of human death.

The silence fell for an instant ... the deadly silence of the battlefield that only signifies new horrors preparing ... then before the new breath could be drawn, a screaming missile whined overhead and ripped through the face of an apartment building across the street. Metalwork and concrete flew in all directions, shattering on the blasted pavement, sending bits of stuff cascading over them.

They watched with tight faces for an instant then, hauling their human burden, slipped quietly and quickly into the evening.

Behind them, the fat shopkeeper lay amidst the debris of his store, dead, safe, and uncaring.

# II

Benno Tallant awoke during the operation, his throat burning with dryness, his
head swimming with fatigue. He saw his
stomach open, the bare organs—slick and
wet in their own pulsing blood—staring up
nakedly at him. A grizzled little man, with
sharp spikes of white beard dotting his
cheeks, was carefully settling a knobbed
and calibrated block of metal into the flesh.
He caught a glimpse of the operating lamp's
idiot glare above him, and promptly fainted
again.

When he awoke the second time, he was
in a cold, cold room, lying naked to the
groin on an operating table, his head
slightly higher than his feet. The red, puck-

9

ered scar that ran from the bottom of his
rib cage to the inside of his thigh stared up
at him. It reminded him of a crimson river
coursing through desert land. The pin-head
gleam of a metal wire-tip stuck up in the
center of the scar. Abruptly, he remembered.

They stopped his screaming by forcing a
wadded towel into his mouth.

The tall blond man from the ruined shop
stepped into Tallant's arc of vision. He had
washed the filth from his face, and he wore
a dun-colored military uniform, with the
triple studs of a Commander on the lapel.
The man stared closely at Tallant for a moment, noting the riot of emotions washing
the looter's face.

"I'm Parkhurst, fellow. Head of Resistance, now that the President and his staff
are dead." He waited for the convulsions of
Tallant's face to cease. They continued, the
eyes growing larger, the skin turning red,
the neck tendons stretching taut.

"We have use for you, mister, but there
isn't much time left . . . so if you want to
stay alive, calm down."

Tallant's face eased into quiet.

They pulled the towel from Benno Tallant's mouth and for a moment his tongue
felt like thick, prickly soup. The picture of
his stomach, split and wet, came back to
him once more. *"What was that?* What have
you done to me? Why do this to me?"* He

was crying; the tears oozed out of the corners of his eyes, running ziggily down his cheeks into the corners of his mouth, and down his chin again.

"I wonder that, too," said a voice from Tallant's left. He turned his head painfully, small shafts of pain hitting him at the base of the neck. He saw the grizzled man with the spiky beard. It was a doctor; the doctor who had been inserting the metal square in Tallant's stomach the first time he had awakened. Tallant assumed this was Doc Budder.

The nearly-bald man continued, "Why this sniveling garbage, Parkhurst? There are a dozen men left in the post who would've volunteered. We would have lost a good man, but at least we'd know the thing was being carried by someone who could do the job."

He caught his breath as he finished speaking; a thick, phlegmy cough made him steady himself on the edge of the operating table. "Too many cigarettes . . ." he managed to gasp out, but Parkhurst helped him to a chair across the room.

Parkhurst shook his head and pointed at Tallant. "The best possible job can be done by somebody who's afraid of the thing. By someone who will run. The running will take time, and that's all that will be left to ensure our living till we get to

11

Earth, or another outpost. What do you think, Doc?

"Do you have any doubt this man will run?"

Doc Budder rubbed the bristling stubble on his chin. It rasped in the silence of the room. "Mmm. I guess you're right, Parkhurst—you usually *are*—it's just that . . ."

Parkhurst cut him off with friendly impatience. "Never mind, Doc. How soon can we have this one up and around?"

Doc Budder wheezingly hoisted himself from the chair. He coughed once more, deeply, said, "I had the epidermizer on him . . . he's knitting nicely. I'll put it back on him but, uh, say, Parkhurst, y'know, all those cigarettes, my nerves are a little jumpy . . . I wonder, uh, would you have a little, uh, something to sort of steady me?" A hopeful gleam appeared in the old man's eyes, and Tallant recognized it at once for what it really was. The old man was a junkie, too. Or a winehead. He couldn't quite tell what, but there was the same unnatural craving eating at Doc Budder that he realized suddenly was eating at him, also.

Parkhurst shook his head firmly. "Nothing, Doc. We have to keep you right on hand in case something goes . . ."

"Goddam it, Parkhurst, I'm not a ward of the state! I'm a doctor, and I have a right to—"

12

Parkhurst turned away from staring at Tallant, staring at Tallant but thinking of Doc Budder. "Look, Doc. This is a bad time for everybody. This is rough on all of us, Doc, but my wife got burned down in the street when the Kyben struck three days ago, and my kids were burned in the school. Now I know it's rough on you, Doc, but if you don't so help me God stop bugging for your whiskey, I'm going to kill you, Doc. I'm going to kill you."

He had spoken softly, pacing his words for full effect and clear understanding, but the desperation in his voice was apparent. The tones of a man with a terrible anguish in him, and a terrible burden on his shoulders. He would not humor the old man any longer.

"Now. How soon can we get him out of here, Doc?"

Doc Budder's eyes swept across the room hopelessly, and his tongue washed his lips. He spoke hurriedly, nervously.

"I'll—I'll put the epidermizer back on it. It should be set in another four hours. There's no weight on the organs; it was a clean insertion. He shouldn't feel a thing."

Benno listened closely. He still didn't know what had been done to him, what the operation had been about, and his overwhelming terror at this whole affair had been sublimated in the little tableau be-

13

tween Budder and Parkhurst. But now he
ran a shaking hand over the scar.

The fear was gagging him, and he felt the
nervous tics starting in his inner upper arm
and his cheek. Doc Budder wheeled a slim,
tentacled machine to the operating table, and
lifted a telescoping arm from the shaft. On
the end was a small rectangular nickel-steel
box with a small hole in it. Budder threw a
switch, and a shaft of light struck out from
the hole, washed the scar.

Even as he watched, the wound seemed
to lose color, pucker more. He couldn't feel
the thing they had put in his stomach, but
he knew it was there.

A sudden cramp hit him.

He cried in pain.

Parkhurst's face turned white. "What's
the matter with him?"

The words came out so quickly, they were
one word.

Doc Budder pushed aside the telescoping
arm of the epidermizer, leaned over Tallant, who lay there breathing with difficulty, his face wrenched into an expression
of utter pain. "What's the matter?"

"It hurts—it—*here*—" He indicated his
stomach. "Pain, all over here, hurts like hell
... *do something!*"

The fat little doctor stepped back with a
sigh. He slapped the telescoping arm back
into position with a careless motion. "It's

all right. Self-induced cramp. I didn't think there'd be any deleterious after-effects.

"But," he added, with a malicious glance at Parkhurst, "I'm not as good a doctor, as sober and upstanding a doctor, as the Resistance could use, if it had its choice, so you never know."

Parkhurst waved a hand in annoyance. "Oh, shut up, Doc."

Doc Budder pulled the sheet up over Tallant's chest, and the looter whined in pain. Budder snarled down at him. "Shut up that goddammed whining, you miserable slug. The machine's healing you through the sheet, you haven't got a thing to worry about ... right now. There are women and kids out there," he waved toward the boarded-up window, "suffering a lot worse than you."

He turned toward the door, Parkhurst following, lines of thought slicing across the blond man's forehead.

Parkhurst stopped with a hand on the knob. "We'll be back with food for you later." He turned back to the door, then added, not looking at Tallant, "Don't try to get out. Aside from the fact that there's a guard on the door—and that's the only way out unless you want to go to *them* through the window—aside from that, you might open that incision and bleed to death before we could find you."

He clicked the light switch, stepped out,

and closed the door behind himself. Tallant heard voices outside the door, softly, as though coming through a blanket of moss, and he knew the guard was standing ready outside.

Tallant's thoughts weren't deterred by the darkness. He remembered the dream-dust, and the pains shot up in him again; he remembered the past, and his mouth chocked up; he remembered awakening during the operation, and he wanted to scream. The darkness did not interfere with Benno Tallant's thoughts.

They became luminous and the next six hours were a bright, thinking hell.

# III

THE LISPING MAN, SHEP, CAME FOR HIM. HE HAD cleaned up, also, but there were fine tracings of dirt around his nose, and under his nails, and in the lines of pocketing beneath his eyes. He had one thing in common with the other men Tallant had seen; he was weary, to the core.

Shep shot the telescoping arm of the epidermizer into its shank-hole, and rolled the machine back against the wall. Tallant watched him carefully, and when Shep turned down the sheet, examining the now-gone thin, white line that had been the incision, Benno raised himself on his elbows, and asked, "How's it going outside?" His tones were friendly, the way a child trying

17

to make up to someone who has been angry with him is friendly.

Shep raised his gray eyes and did not answer.

He left the room, reappeared a few minutes later with a bundle of clothes. He threw them on the operating table next to Tallant, and helped the looter sit up. "Get dressed," he said shortly.

Tallant sat up, and for a moment the crawling of his belly-hunger for the dream-dust made him gag. He hung his head down and opened his mouth, making retching noises deep in his throat. But he was nausea-dry, and nothing came.

He straightened up and put a shaking hand through his brown hair. "L-listen," he began, speaking confidentially to the Resistance man, "do y-you know where I can lay my hands on some dream-dust? I-I can make it worth your while, I've got—"

Shep turned on him, and the lisping man's hand slammed against Tallant's face, leaving a burning red mark. "No, mister, *you* listen to *me*. In case you don't know it, there's a Kyban battle armada on its way across space, headed directly for Deald's World. We've only been hit by an advance scout party, and they've nearly demolished the planet as it is.

"About two million people are dead out there, buddy. Do you know how many peo-

18

ple that is? That's almost the entire popu-
lation of this planet.

"And you sit there asking me to get you
your snuff!

"If I had any say in the matter, I'd kick
you to death right here, right now.

"Now you get into those goddammed
clothes, and don't say another word to me,
or so help me God I'm not responsible for
what happens to you!"

He turned away, and Tallant stared after
him. There was no fight in him, merely a
desire to lie down and cry. Why was this
happening to him? He'd try anything to get
the dust now . . . it was getting bad inside
him . . . real bad . . . and he'd tried to stay
out of the fighting . . . he'd only been getting
the money from that shop to find a pusher
. . . why were they badgering him . . . what
had they *done* to him?

"*Get dressed!*" Shep shouted, the cords in
his neck tightening, his face screwing into
an expression of rage.

Tallant hurriedly slipped into the jumper
and hood, the boots, and buckled the belt
around himself.

"Come on." Shep prodded him off the table.

Tallant stood up, nearly fell, he clung to
Shep in terror, feeling the unsteadiness
washing through him.

Shep shrugged his hands off, com-

19

manded, "Walk, you slimy, yellow bastard! *Walk!*"

He walked, and they went down the hall, into another sealed-tight compartment, and Tallant realized they must be underground.

He walked slightly behind Shep, knowing there was no place else to go, and the lisping man seemed to pay him no attention; knowing the looter would follow.

Through the walls—and through the very ground, Tallant estimated—he could hear the reverberations of shock bombs hitting the planet. He knew only vaguely what was happening.

The Earth-Kyban War had been a long and costly battle—they had been fighting for sixteen years—but this was the first time a Kyban fleet had broken through this far into the Terran dominion.

But it had obviously been a sudden, sneak attack, and Deald's World was the first planet to be hit. He had seen the devastation, while aboveground, and he knew that if these men were alive and working to defend Deald's World, they were the last pocket of the Resistance left.

But what did they want with him?

Shep turned right down a corridor, and palmed a loktite open. He stepped aside and Tallant walked into what appeared to be a communications room.

High banks of dials and switches, tubes and speaker rigs covered the walls. Park-

20

hurst was there, holding a hand-mike care-lessly, talking to a technician.

The blond man turned as Tallant stepped through. He nodded to himself, as though setting everything right in his mind, as though satisfied that all was going as planned, now that the looter was here. "We thought you'd like to know what this is all about." He hesitated. "We owe you that, at any rate."

The technician waved his hand in a circle, one finger extended, indicating they had started something turning, perhaps indicat-ing the batteries were being warmed.

Parkhurst pursed his lips for a moment, then said almost apologetically, "We don't hate you, fellow." Tallant realized that they had not even bothered to find out his name yet. "We have a job to do," Parkhurst con-tinued, half-watching Tallant, half-watching the technician, "and more is at stake than you or me or the life of anyone left here on Deald's World. Much more.

"We had a job to do, and for the job we needed a certain type of man. You fit the bill so beautifully, you'll never quite know. There was no premeditation; it just hap-pened to be you. If it hadn't been you, it would have been someone *like* you." He shrugged with finality.

Tallant felt the shivers beginning. He stood quaking, wishing he had just a sniff of the dust, just a miserable sniff. He wasn't

21

interested in all this high-flown patriotic gabble Parkhurst was throwing at him; all he wanted was to be let alone, let back out there, even if the Kyben *were* burning the planet, just to get back out there. Perhaps he could find a cache of the dust ... because he knew he wouldn't get it from these men. If Doc Budder couldn't get his hootch, then they wouldn't give Tallant any dream-dust.

Yes, that was it. He knew it now. It was a plot, a conspiracy to keep him from his beloved dust. He had to have it, he was *going* to have it—but he would wait, he would be sly and cautious, and wait till these mad-men were out of the way, till they weren't watching, then he would get away. There were no Kyben aboveground, it was only a foul, despicable plot to keep him from his beloved dust. His eyes narrowed.

Then the memory of the metal thing in his stomach jerked him instantly to reality. Tallant stood quaking. He had still not got-ten over his terror at seeing the metal thing placed in his stomach.

His sallow face was dotted with sweat and streaked with dirt, though they had washed him several times during the six hours it had taken the scar to heal.

He was a lean man; the gray tuberous sort of man who always brings the wolf or pack-rat to mind. Brown hair and small, deep-set eyes. A face that seemed to taper to a rodentlike tip.

"What—what are you going to do with me now?" He touched himself lightly, almost fearfully, on the stomach. "What is that thing you did to me?"

A high, keening whine broke from one of the many speakers on the wall, and the tight-lipped technician gestured wildly at Parkhurst, finally tapping him on the shoulder. Parkhurst turned to the technician, and the man gave him a go-ahead signal. Parkhurst motioned Tallant to silence, motioned Shep to stand close by the shaking looter.

Then he spoke into the hand-mike. A bit too clearly, a bit too loudly, as though he were speaking to someone a great distance away, as though he wanted every word precise and easily understood.

"This is the headquarters of Resistance on Deald's World. We are subjects of Earth, and we are speaking to the Kyban fleet.

"Are you listening? This call is being broadcast over all tight beams, so we are certain you receive us. We'll wait ten minutes for you to rig up a translator and to hook in with your superiors, so they can hear this announcement.

"This is of vital importance to you Kyban, so we suggest as soon as you've translated what I've just said, you make the proper arrangements, and contact your officers."

He signaled the technician to cut off.

Then Parkhurst once again turned to Tallant. "They'll translate. They'll have to . . . they knew the best way to attack, so they must have had contact with Earth Traders, or Terran ships that went too far into the Coalsack. They will be able to decipher us."

Tallant ran a thin hand up his neck. "What are you going to do with me? What are you going to do?" He felt hysteria building in him, but could not stop the flow of words. *He was afraid!* "This isn't fair! You've got to tell me!" His voice became shrill. Shep moved in closer behind him, clasped the looter's arm above the elbow. Tallant stopped just as another torrent of words was about to burst forth.

Parkhurst spoke unhurriedly, quietly, trying to calm Tallant. "This is the advance guard of a gigantic Kyban fleet, mister. We're sure of that because there are almost fifty ships in the force that attacked us. If that's what they are using for an advance scout, the fleet must be the largest assembled during the War.

"It's obvious they intend to crush right through, the sheer force of weight breaking through all the Earth defenses, and perhaps strike at Earth itself.

"This is the big push of the War for the Kyben, and there is no way to get word to

24

Earth. Our inverspace transmitters went when they burned down the transpoles at the meridian. There's no way to warn the home planet. They're defenseless if all the outer colonies go—as they surely will if this fleet gets through.

"We've got to warn Earth. And the only way we can do it, and with luck save the lives of the few thousands left alive on Deald's World, is to stall for time. That's why we needed a man like you. You."

Then he fell silent, and they waited silently.

The only sounds in the room were the click and whisper of the blank-faced machines, the tight, sobbing breaths of Benno Tallant.

Finally the big wall-chronometer had ticked away ten minutes, and the technician signaled Parkhurst once more.

The blond man took up the hand-mike again, and began speaking quietly, earnestly, knowing he was no longer dealing with subordinates, but the men in power up there above the planet; speaking as though each word were the vital key to a great secret.

"We have placed a bomb on this planet. A sun-bomb. I'm sure you know what that means. The entire atmosphere will heat, right up to the top layers of the stratosphere. Not quite enough to turn this world into a nova, but well enough above the point

25

where every living thing will perish, every bit of metal heat to incandescence, the ground scorched through till nothing can ever grow again. This world, all of us, all of *you*, will die.

"Most of your fifty ships have landed. The few that remain in the sky can not hope to escape the effects of this bomb, even if they leave now. And if they do—you are being tracked by radar—we will set the bomb off without a moment's hesitation. If you wait, there is another possibility open to you."

He tossed a glance at the technician, whose eyes were fixed on a bank of radar screens with one pip in the center of each. The technician shook his head, and Tallant realized they were waiting to see if their story was accepted. If one of those pips moved out away from the planet, it would mean the Kyben did not believe, or thought it was a bluff.

But the Kyben obviously could not chance it. The pips remained solidly fastened to the center of the screens.

Then Tallant's eyes suddenly widened. What Parkhurst had said was finally penetrating. He *knew* what the blond man meant! He *knew* where that bomb was hidden. He started to scream, but Shep's hand was over his mouth before the sound could escape, could go out over the transmitter to the Kyben.

He became violently ill. Shep drew away

from him, cursing softly, pulling a rag from a console top to wipe himself off. Tallant continued to vomit in dry, wracking heaves, and Shep moved back swiftly to catch him as he fell.

The lisping man sat Tallant down on a console bench, and continued daubing at his spattered uniform.

Tallant knew he was on the verge of madness.

He had lived by his wits all his life, and it had always been the little inch someone would allow him that had afforded the miles he had attained. But there was no inch this time. Bewildered, he realized he could not take advantage of the weakness or the politeness of these men, as he had taken advantage of so many others. These men were hard, and ruthless, and they had planted a sun-bomb—My God In Heaven!—a *sun*-bomb in his stomach!

He had once seen stereos of a sun-bomb explosion.

He threw up again, this time falling to the floor.

Through a fog he heard Parkhurst continue: "We repeat, don't try to take off. If we see one of your ships begin to blast, we'll trigger the bomb. We give you one alternative to total destruction. To destruction of this planet you will need so desperately for storage, refueling and supply for your fleet. One alternative."

He paused, looked around the communications room, which had suddenly seemed to grow so crowded. He seemed a bit embarrassed, perhaps by the obvious histrionics of the tense situation. Parkhurst licked his lips and went on carefully, "Let us go. Let the Earthmen on this planet blast away, and we promise not to set off the bomb. After we have left the atmosphere, we will set the bomb on automatic, and leave it for you to find yourselves. If you doubt we have actually done as I say, take a stabilization count with whatever instruments you have to detect neutrino emission.

"That should convince you instantly that *this is no bluff!*

"We will tell you this, however. There is one way the bomb may be deactivated. You can find it in time, but not till we have gotten away. It is a gamble you will *have* to take. The other way . . . there is no gamble at all. Only death.

"If you don't comply, we set off the bomb. If you do accede to our demands, we will leave at once, and the bomb will be set to automatic, and will go off at a designated time. It's set with a foolproof time-device, and it can't be damped by any neutrino-dampers.

"That is our conditioned demand. We'll wait for your answer no more than an hour.

At the end of that time, we trigger the bomb, even if we are to die!

"You can reach us over the band on which you are receiving this message."

He motioned to the technician, who threw a switch. A bank of lights went dark, and the transmitter was dead.

Parkhurst turned to Tallant, lying shivering in his own filth. His eyes were very sad, and very tired. He had to say something, and it was obvious what he said would be cruel, terrifying.

*Don't let him say it, don't let him say it, don't let him say it,* Benno Tallant kept repeating in the maddened confines of his mind. He screwed his eyes shut, put his slippery fists to them to ensure the darkness, perhaps blotting out what Parkhurst would say.

But the blond man spoke.

"Of course," he said quietly, "that end of it *may* be a bluff. I may be lying. There may *not* be any way to damp that bomb. Even after they find it."

29

# IV

TALLANT HAD BEEN IN SUCH BAD SHAPE, THEY
had had to lock him in the operating room,
after removing everything breakable. Shep
had been for strapping Tallant to the table,
but Parkhurst and the pig-faced man—an
ex-baker turned sniper named Banneman—
were against it.

They left Benno Tallant in the room,
while the hour elastically drew itself out.
Finally, Shep palmed the loktite open and
came in to find the looter lying on his side
in the room, his legs drawn up near his
chest, his hands down over his knees, the
wide, dark eyes staring unseeingly at the
limp, relaxed fingers.

He drew a pitcherful of water from a tap

in the next room, and threw it on Tallant's face. The looter came out of his almost trancelike state with a wail and a start. He looked up, and memories flooded back at once. And the dust hunger.

"J-just a sniff . . . just a s-sniff is all I want . . . *please!*"

Shep stared at the weakling with a mixture of disgust and livid hopelessness. "*This* is the savior of Earth!" He spat on the floor.

Tallant's guts were untwisting. His mouth was dry then foully wet then dry again. His head ached and his muscles were constricted. He wanted that dust more than anything, he *had* to have it. They had to *help* him. He whined, and crawled toward Shep's boots.

The lisping man drew back. "Get on your feet. They expect the answer any minute."

Tallant got to his feet painfully, steadying himself on the operating table. They had the table bolted to the floor, but he had managed to bend two of its legs in his frantic, screaming drive to get out, to get to the dust.

"Come on," he said.

Shep led the shivering, drooling Tallant to the communications room once more, and when Parkhurst saw the state of disintegration coming over Tallant, he spoke quietly to Doc Budder. The spike-chinned old man nodded, and slipped past Tallant, out the door. Tallant stared around the room with blank eyes, till Doc Budder came back.

The old man held a snow-white packet, and Tallant recognized it for what it was. Dream-dust. "Gimme, gimme, gimme, please, ya gotta give it to me, give it, give me . . ."

He extended shaking, pale hands, and his twitching fingers sought the packet. Doc Budder, recognizing another addict was getting his craving, while *he* suffered without his own poison, held the packet back, taunting Tallant for a moment.

The addict struggled toward the old man, almost fell on him, his breath ragged and drool slipping out of his mouth. "Gimme, gimme, gimme, gimme . . ." His voice was a whisper, fervent, pleading.

The Doc laughed shrilly, enjoying the game, but Parkhurst snapped, "Let him alone, Doc. I said let him have his dope!"

The Doc threw the packet to the floor, and Tallant was on hands and knees in an instant, scrabbling for it. He had it in his hands, and he ripped the packet open with his teeth.

He struggled across the floor on his knees, to the comm-console and ripped a piece of paper from a pad. He folded it one time, and let the white dream-dust filter out of the packet, into the trough of paper.

Then he turned to the wall, crouching down so they could not see what he was doing, and inhaled the dust through each nostril.

Even as the dust slid up his nasal passages, the hunger died, the strength returned to him, the pressure eased from the base of his skull, his hands stopped trembling.

When he turned back he was no longer a shambles.

He was only a coward.

"How much longer?" Banneman asked from across the room, carefully keeping his eyes from Tallant.

"Any minute now," the technician answered from behind his commask. And as though his words had been a signal, the squawk-boxes made a static sound, and the rasp of a translating machine broke the silence of the room.

It was in a cold, metallic voice, product of changing Kyban to English.

"We accept. You have the bomb, as our instruments indicate, so we allow you seven hours to load and leave." That was the message, that was all.

But Tallant's heart dropped in his body. If the alien instruments showed an increase in neutrino emission, it could only mean his last hope was gone. The Resistance *did* have the bomb, and he knew where it was.

He was a walking bomb. He was walking death!

34

"Let's get moving," Parkhurst said, and started toward the corridor.

"What about me?" Tallant's voice rose again and he grasped at Parkhurst's sleeve. "Now that they'll let us go, you don't need me any more, do you? You can take that— that *thing* out of me!"

Parkhurst looked at Tallant wearily, an edge of sadness in his eyes. "Take care of him, Shep. We'll need him, seven hours from now." And he was gone.

Tallant remained with Shep, as the others left. He turned to the lisping man, and cried out, "What? Tell me! What?"

Then Shep explained it all to Tallant.

"You're going to be the last man on Deald's World. Those Kyban have tracing machines to circle down on centers of neutrino emission. They would find it in a moment if it were in one place. But a moving human being isn't always in one place. They'll never suspect it's in a human being.

"They'll think we're all gone. But you'll still be here, with the bomb. You're our insurance policy.

"Parkhurst controls the bomb as long as he's on the planet, and it won't go off. But as soon as he leaves, he sets it on automatic, and it goes off in the time allotted to it.

"That way, if an alien ship tries to follow us, tries to take off, the bomb explodes. If

35

they *don't* take off, and don't find it in time,
it goes off anyhow.''

He was so cool in explaining, so uncaring
that he was condemning Tallant to death,
that Benno Tallant felt the strength of his
dream-dust rising in him, felt anguish and
fury at being used as a dupe and a walking
bomb.

"What if I just turn myself in to them and
let them cut it out with surgery, the same
way you put it in?" Tallant snapped, with
momentary bravery.

"You won't," Shep answered smugly.

"Why not?"

"Because they won't bother being as gen-
tle as we were. The first detachment of Kyban foot-soldiers that trace the bomb to you
will pin you to the ground and let an atta-
ché slice you open."

He watched the horror that passed
across Tallant's face. "You see, the longer
you keep running, the longer it takes them
to find you. And the longer it takes them to
find you, the better chance we have of getting back to warn Earth. So we had to pick
a man who was so stinking cowardly, he
would keep running . . . because his whole
nature depended on running . . . on staying
alive.

"No, you'll keep running, fellow. That's
why Parkhurst picked you. You'll run, mister, and never stop!"

36

Tallant drew himself up, and *screamed*, "My name is Tallant. Benno Tallant. Do you understand I have a name! I'm Tallant, Benno, Benno, Benno, Tallant!"

Shep grinned nastily and slumped down on the console bench. "I don't give a flying damn *what* your name is, fellow. Why do you think we never asked you your name?

"Without a name, you'll be all the easier to forget. This isn't an easy thing to do—for Parkhurst and the others—they have feelings and scruples about you, fellow.

"But I don't. A dream-duster just like you assaulted my wife before—before—" He stopped, and his eyes raised to the ceiling. Aboveground the Kyben sat, waiting. "So I sort of figure it all evens out. I don't mind seeing a dustie like you die, at all. Not at all."

Tallant made a break for the door, then, but Shep had his rifle up, and a sharp crack slammed it into the small of Benno Tallant's back. The looter slumped to the floor, writhing in pain, crying out.

Shep slipped back to his seat.

"Now we'll just wait about seven hours," he said quietly. "Then you become real valuable, fellow. Real valuable. Y'know, you've got the life of the Kyban fleet in your belly."

He laughed, and laughed some more, and Benno Tallant thought he would go mad

37

from the sounds of underground laughter. He just wanted to lie down. And die.

But that would come later.

The rocket field was silent at last. The noise of loading the few remaining thousands of Dealders had crashed back and forth for seven hours, and the ships had gone up in great clouds of fumes and exhaust trailings. Now the last ship was finished, and Benno Tallant watched as Parkhurst lifted the little girl. She was a tiny girl with yellow braids, and she clutched a plastic toy. Parkhurst held her an instant longer than necessary, staring at her face; and Tallant saw compassion and sorrow for his own dead children coursing across the blond man's face. But he felt no sympathy for Parkhurst.

They were leaving him here to die in the most frightening way possible.

Parkhurst hoisted the little girl, set her inside the ship's plug-port, where the other hands received her. He began to swing up himself.

He paused with one hand on the swing-rail. He turned and looked at Tallant, standing with shaking hands at his sides, like a lost dog, pleading not to be left behind.

It was difficult for him, Tallant could tell. The man was not a murderer; he felt this was the only possible solution to the problem. He had to warn Earth. But Tallant could feel no companionship. My God! They were condemning him to turn into a sun . . .

"Look, mister, it's like this. We're not as stupid as the Kyben think. They assume we'll blast and leave the bomb here. We'll be in our pokey little ships, they'll find and damp the bomb, then take off and wipe us out somewhere in space. All canned and ready to be burned.

"But they're wrong, Tallant. We made sure they wouldn't find that bomb.

"In time, with their neutrino-detectors, they could get the sun-bomb. But not if the carrier is moving. We *had* to find a man like you, Tallant. A coward, a runner.

"You're the only assurance we have that we'll make it to an Earth outpost to warn the mother world. I—I can't say anything to you that will make you think any better of us; don't you think I've burned over and over in my mind for what I'm doing? Get that look off your face, and say something!"

Tallant stared silently ahead, the fear draining down and around in him like poison rotting his legs.

"Somehow, even though I know you'll die, and I know I'm sentencing you to death, I look on you with pride. Can you understand anything as strange as that, mister? Can you understand that even though I've used the life in you the way I'd use the power of a robot-truck, I'm prideful because I *know* you will keep them away from you for a long, long time, and I will be able to save these few people left, save the Earth.

"Can you understand that?"

Tallant broke. He grabbed Parkhurst's sleeve. "Oh, please, please, in the name of God, take me with you! Don't leave me here! I'll die ... I'll ... die ..."

Parkhurst disengaged Tallant's hand quickly, his face tense.

Tallant fell back. "But why? Why do you hate me? Why do you want me to die?" Sobs caught in the looter's throat.

The Resistance leader's face became grim. "No, don't *think* that! Please, don't think that! I didn't even know you when we found we needed a man like you for this, mister. I hate your type, that's true, but there's no reason for me to hate *you!*

"You're a hero, mister. When—if—we get through this, a monument will be set up for you. It's no good, and it won't help you, but it will be set up.

"In the past seven hours I've schooled myself to despise you. I have to, mister, or I'd never leave you here. I'd stay in your stead, but that would do no good. I wouldn't have the same desire to run. I'm tired; my wife, my kids, they're all dead. *I* want to die, I just want to die. But, but, *you*—you want to live, and you'll run till they can't

40

find you, and that will give us the time we need!

"I've taught myself to think of you as some sort of refuse of the human race.

"And," he added, in frantic justification, "you've helped me think of you that way. Look at yourself!"

Tallant knew what Parkhurst meant. He *was* garbage, he *was* a coward, he *would* run. He could almost picture his own slight body shaking as though under an ague, the sweat rolling off him, the fear a live thing around his body, his eyes large and white-ringed as they looked for a way out. Tallant knew he was a coward. It didn't help any.

He didn't want to die like this!

"So," Parkhurst finished, "I hate you because I *have* to hate you, mister. And because I hate you, because I hate myself, and *not* you, I've done this to you. And because you are what you are, you'll run and hide from those Kyban so that we can get to a relay station, and warn Earth they're coming."

He began to swing up into the ship again, when Tallant once more clutched his arm.

The coward had pleaded all through these last hours, and even now he knew no other way. A lifetime of sowing had reaped him a harvest of spinelessness.

"At least, at least tell me, *is* there a way to damp the bomb. Can it be done? You told

41

*them* that it could!" The childish eagerness of his expression caused Parkhurst's face to wrinkle with disgust.

"There isn't a bone in your body, is there?"

"Answer me! *Tell me!*" Tallant shouted. Faces appeared whitely at the ports of the spaceship.

"I can't tell you, mister. If there were, if you knew for certain, you'd be off to the Kyban lines right now. But if you think it'll go off when they touch it, you'll wait a long time." He shook the man's hand loose and pulled himself up into the ship.

The port began to slide home, and Parkhurst stopped it for a second, his voice softening as he said:

"I know you. Goodbye, Benno Tallant. I wish I could say God bless you."

The port slid shut. Tallant could hear it being dogged, and the whine of the atomic motors starting up. He ran away from the blast area in wild blindness, seeking the protection of the bunkers set back from the blast pit. The bunkers beneath which the Resistance had their headquarters.

He stood at the filtered window, watching the thin line of exhaust trailings disappearing into the night sky.

He was alone.

The last man on Deald's World.

He remembered what Parkhurst had said:

*I don't hate you. But this has to be done. It has to be done, and you will have to do it. But I don't hate you.*

And here he was, alone with a planet of attacking Kyben he had never even seen, and a total destruction bomb in his stomach.

# V

AFTER THEY WERE GONE, AFTER THE LAST DROP of exhaust trail had been lost in the starry night sky, Tallant stood by the open door of the bunker, staring across the emptiness of the field. They had left him; all his begging, all his appeals to their humanity, all his struggling, all of it had been for nothing. He was lost, lost out here in space, with the emptiness of the field and the emptiness of his heart.

The chill winds from the ocean came rippling across the field, caught him in their wake, and smoothed over him. He felt the hunger rising once more.

But this time, if nothing else, he could drown himself in dream-dust. That was it!

He would send himself into a dust stupor, and lie there in heaven till the bomb went off, killing him.

He found the trapdoor, lifted it, and went down into the Resistance headquarters.

A half hour, throwing supplies around, smashing into lockers, breaking open cabinets, and he had found Doc Budder's supply of medicinal dream-dust. Nurmoheroinyte concentrate; the dream-dust that had found him, made him a slave after one small sampling when he was twenty-three years old. That had been a long time before this, and he knew this was his only rest now.

He sniffed away a packet, and felt himself getting stronger, healthier, more fierce. Kyben? Yes, bring them on! He could fight the entire armada single-handed. *Then* let those lousy sonofabitching Earthies try to come back. Deald's World would be his, he would be the king, the master of the universe!

He strutted back up the stairs, slammed back the trapdoor, the white packets in his jumper pocket.

Tallant saw his first Kyben then.

They were swarming across the rocket field, hundreds of them. They were average-sized, more than five feet tall, less than six, all of them. They looked almost human—only golden-skinned, and their fingers ended in silky tentacles, six of them to a hand.

Abruptly, the resemblance to normal humans terrified Tallant. Had they been grotesque, it would be something else; he could despise and hate them as monsters. But these Kyben were, if anything, handsomer than humans.

He had never seen them before, but he had heard the screams that had echoed through the city's canyons. He had heard a girl getting the flesh flayed off her back, and in his own way he had felt sorry for her. He remembered he had wished she might die from loss of blood. Wounds like that would only take three or four hours to kill her. With the Kyben, that would have been the quickest, least painful way.

Yet they looked very much like humans. But golden.

Suddenly Tallant realized he was trapped. He was caught in one of the bunkers, with no protection, no weapon, no way out. They would find him, and kill him, not realizing he had the bomb in him. They would not ask whether or not he carried a bomb . . . that was too ridiculous to consider.

That was why Parkhurst had done it. It was too ridiculous to consider.

They were looking for a sun-bomb, and that bomb—according to the logic of a searcher—would be in some obscure hiding place. In the ocean, under a thousand tons of dirt, in a cave. But not in a human being. A human being was the last thing they might consider.

Nobody could be cruel enough to plant a sun-bomb in a human being.

That was why Parkhurst had done it.

He looked around the bunker wildly. There was only the one exit. And the field was crawling with Kyben—furious enough at having been outfoxed to gut the first Earthie they found.

He watched them getting larger and larger in the filtered window.

As he watched, he noticed something further about them. They all wore suits of insulating mail, and each carried a triple-thread blastick. They were armed to kill, not to capture prisoners. He was trapped!

Tallant felt the fury of desperation welling up in him again. As it had when he had first learned he carried the sun-bomb. Not only to be boxed-in this way—to be a human bomb—but to have to keep running. He knew the Kyben were ruthless. They would already have started scouting for the bomb with ship-based emission detectors, spiraling over the planet in ever-decreasing circles, narrowing in on the bomb.

When they found it was not stationary, they would know it was in a living carrier. They would close in relentlessly, then. He was trapped!

But if these common foot-soldiers on the field got to him, he wouldn't even get *that* far, far enough to run. They would scorch him and laugh over his charred carcass. If they had that long to laugh. The bomb was certain to go off if he died—Parkhurst had said as much.

He had to get away.

Parkhurst was right. The only escape was in flight.

If he could stay alive long enough, he might be able to figure a way of dampening the bomb himself.

Or he had to keep away from them long enough to get to the Kyban commanding officers. It was the only chance. If he kept running, and avoided them entirely—the bomb would detonate eventually. He had to get to the men in charge, and have *them* remove the bomb without triggering it.

He would outsmart Parkhurst and his filthy bunch of survivors. He would not *let* himself get caught, unless it was by the right persons, in high places. Then he would offer his services to the Kyban, and help them hunt down the Earthmen, and kill them.

After all, what did he owe Earth?

Nothing. Nothing at all. They had tried to kill him, and he would make them pay. He would *not* die! He would live with his beloved dream-dust forever. Forever!

If he could remain alive that long, he would be able to think his way out of the Kyban camp. *That* was the answer!

Yes, that was it.

But now one Kyban foot-soldier was

dodging, broken-field running, and now he was at the door of the bunker, and now he was inside, his triple-thread blastick roaring, spraying flame and death around the bunker.

Tallant had been beside the window, behind the door. Now he slammed the door, so the others on the field could not see what was happening, and he found a new strength, a strength he had not known he possessed.

He dove low from behind the Kyban soldier, tackling him. The soldier fell, the blastick jarred from his hands, and Benno Tallant was up, stamping the man's face in. One, two, three, four and the man was dead, his head a pulped mass.

Then Tallant knew what to do.

He dragged the soldier by his feet to the edge of the trapdoor, lifted it, and shoved the man through. The body went clattering down the stairs, and landed with a thump.

Tallant grabbed up the blastick and slipped in before any more soldiers could appear. He let the trapdoor slam shut, knowing it would not be seen unless there was a thorough search; there was no reason to expect that, as they believed all Earthmen had left the planet. This was a reconnaissance mission, and there would be no search.

He desperately hoped.

He crouched down, beneath the trapdoor,

the blastick ready in his hands, ready to smear off the face of anyone who lifted the door.

Overhead he heard the sound of shouts, and the door of the bunker crashed open against the wall. He heard the rasp and roar of more blasticks being fired, and then the sound of voices in the sibilant hiss of the Kyban tongue. He heard boots stomping around above him, and men searching. Once a foot stepped directly on the trapdoor, and little bits of dust and dirt filtered through around the edges, and he thought he was caught then.

But a shout from outside brought grudging answer from the men, and they trooped out, leaving the bunker deserted.

Tallant lifted the door to make certain, and when he saw it was clear, lifted it higher to look through the filtered window. The Kyben were moving off in the other direction.

He decided to wait till they had gone. Night was upon the land, and he wanted to get away.

While he waited, he sniffed a packet of dust.

He was God again!

He made it as far as the Blue Marshes before another patrol found him.

He had been moving—unawares—in the most perfect escape pattern imaginable,

51

circling outward, so that any Kyban ships tracking overhead with emission detectors could not pinpoint him. Eventually, of course, they would see that the target was not in the same place, and then they would recognize what the Earthmen had done.

He kept moving.

It was a totally cloudless, moonless night, with the stark black tips of the Faraway Mountains rising up beyond the marsh clingers and vines. The smell of the night was clean and quick, till he stepped off the land, and entered the Marshes. Then all the rot of the eternities swam up to offend his nostrils.

Tallant's stomach heaved, and for a moment he wondered if vomiting would set the bomb off. Then he recalled having been sick before, and knew action of that sort could not trigger the weapon.

He stepped into the swirling, sucking blue-black mud, and instantly felt it dragging down, down at his boots. He lifted the blastick above his head for leverage, and stepped high, pulling up each foot with a muted, sucking *thwup!* as he slowly moved.

The Marshes were filled with animal life, and whether vicious or harmless, they all made their voices heard. The noises swelled as he trod deeper into the dankness, as though some unimaginable insect telegraphy was warning the inhabitants that outside life was approaching. Ahead of him, and slightly to the left, he heard the deep-throated roar of a beast, and he knew it was big.

The fear began to ring his belly once more, and he found himself muttering, "Why me?" over and over again, in a dull monotone that somehow helped him keep going. As he moved, the subtle phosphorescence of the blue-black muck swirled, coating his lower legs and boots with glowing tips, and each step left a moment's round-edged hole in the stuff. Which was quickly sucked closed.

It was as he was scrambling over a rotted stump, fallen across the open way, having set his blastick in the crotch of a bush on the other side, that the beast broke out of the clinging matted vines, and trumpeted its warning at him.

Tallant froze. One foot in the air, the other shoved into a niche in the stump, his hands holding his full weight. His eyes opened wide, and he saw the dark gray bulk of the animal all at once.

It was almost triangular. A smooth front rose up to an almost idiotically tiny head, set at the apex of the triangle. The back was a long slope that tapered down to the ground. Its eight legs were set under it, almost as a kickplate might be set under a bookcase.

Two tiny red eyes gleamed through the mist of the Blue Marshes, set above a

square snout and a fanged mouth that slob-
bered ooze. The beast stood silent for a moment. Then muted coughs left its throat,
and its imbecilic head rose an inch on the
non-existent neck.

It sniffed the breeze, it sniffed the mist, it
sniffed the spoor of Benno Tallant. It took
one step, two, faltering, as though trying to
decide whether advance was recom-
mended. Tallant stared at the animal, unable to move himself from its path, a cold
wash of complete terror hingeing him to the
stump as if it were the one solid form in
the universe.

The beast trumpeted again, and lum-
bered forward.

Its scream struck out into the night, and
the blast of fire that ripped at its gray hide
came from nowhere. The beast rose up on
its back sets of legs, pawing at the sky. Another *scheeee* of power and the flames bit
at the animal's tiny head.

For an instant the thing was wrapped in
flame and smoke, then it exploded outward.
Blood spilled through the leaves and vines, covering Tallant with warm, sticky nausea. Bits of
flesh cascaded down, and he felt one slippery
bit go sliding down his cheek.

His stomach twisted painfully in him, but
the explosion unstuck him. He was not
alone in the Marshes.

Since he was the last *man* on Deald's
World, there was only one other answer.

Kyben? *Kyben!*

Then he heard their voices above the trembling sounds of the Marshes. They were around a bank of bushy trees, about to burst into the clearing where the scattered hulk of the beast lay, quivering, even in death.

Tallant felt a strange quivering in himself. He found a sudden inexplicable identification with the beast, lying out there in the open. That beast had been more man than he. It had died, in its brutishness, but it had not turned and run away. He knew the animal had no mind, and yet there was something . . . *something* . . . in the beast's death that made him feel altered, changed, matured. He could never tell what it had been, but when the animal had died, he knew he would never give up to the Kyben. He was still terribly frightened—the habits of a lifetime could not change in a moment—but there was a difference now. If he was going to die, he was going to make sure he died on his feet—not in the back as he ran away.

The Kyben came into view. They moved out from his left, almost close enough for him to touch them. They moved across the clearing, and he knew they had not seen him. But they had mechanisms that could trace the bomb's emissions, and in a few moments they would get his track. He had to do something—and quickly.

The five Kyben moved to the dead animal, obviously too engrossed in examining their kill to study their detectors. Tallant reached for the blastick in the crotch of the tree.

He slipped on the stump, and his hand collided with the metal of the weapon. It clattered free from the tree, and fell with a splash into the mud.

One of the Kyben whirled, saw Tallant, and screamed something softly deadly to his companions, bringing his own instrument up. A blast of blue power streaked through the space between them, and Tallant hesitated only an instant. It was almost an instant too long. The blast-beam seared across his back, barely touching him, ripping wide his jumper's covering, scorching his flesh.

He screamed in agony, and dove headfirst into the muck himself, both trying to extinguish the fires of hell that arched on his back, and trying to find the weapon that had disappeared into the mire.

He fell solidly into the stuff, and felt it closing over his head. It was a pool of mud deeper than he had thought.

The stuff clogged his throat, and he struck out blindly. His hands broke top, and he suddenly realized this might be his only way out.

He tried to reach bottom, found it with his flailing feet, and dragged himself across the pool, gagging with each step. He felt the

56

land rising under him, and stuck his head out momentarily.

The Kyben were still in front of him, but they were turned away slightly, thinking he was still in the same position, that perhaps he had drowned.

He knew immediately that he had to kill them all, and before they could call in to their superiors, or the game was up. The moment the Kyban Command knew there was a human left on the planet, they would realize where the bomb was hidden. Then any chance he had of surviving was gone.

He saw one of the Kyben—a tallish one with golden hair clipped into an extremely exaggerated flattop—turning toward him, his blastick at the ready. Then the adrenaline pumped through Tallant's veins, and he saw the beast, and for the first time in his life—knowing the dream-dust had worn off, but not really caring—he moved with aggression. He started running.

Lifting his feet high, he pounded around the rim of the pool, spraying blue mud and slime in every direction. The suddenness of the movement surprised the Kyban, and he failed to bring the blastick into play.

In a moment, Tallant was on him, the drive of his rushing advance bowling the Kyban over. Tallant's foot came down with a snap, and he felt the alien's neck snap under the pressure of his boot.

Then he had the blastick in his arms,

57

fumbling for the fire stud, and raw power was blueing out, in a wide arc, catching the remaining four members of the patrol.

Their screams were short, and their bodies spattered the Marshes for fifty feet. Tallant stared down at the raw, pulsing husks that had been men a minute before, and leaned against a tree.

*God, God, God* . . . he murmured over and over in his mind's desertland, and felt the nausea rising again. He thought of the dust for a moment. Of the packets in his sealed jumper pocket, but felt no need for it now.

Somehow, the fire was up in him.

The killer instinct was rising in the coward.

Tallant struck out again, a fresh weapon in his hands.

By now the Earthmen were far away in their ships, and the Kyben still feared the bomb would trigger if they tried to take off; Tallant *knew* they had not tried to leave Deald's World by one fact only:

The bomb in his middle had not exploded yet.

But time was dripping away.

# VI

THAT NIGHT, TALLANT KILLED HIS TWENTIETH and thirtieth Kyben.

The second set of five went as he left the Blue Marshes. Ambushed from behind a huge, snout-like rock, they went down bubbling.

Single reconnaissance men died by knife and by club at Tallant's hands as he made his way through the fields of swaying, unharvested Summerset that lay on the outskirts of Xville. They walked slowly through the fields, another five-man team, just their shoulders and heads showing above the tall burnished stalks of grain. Occasionally Tallant, from where he crouched below sight-level in the field, saw the snout of a blastick poke up from the Summerset. It was hardly difficult at all to drag each man down in his turn as the alien passed nearby.

The first one's skull shattered like a plastic carton, as Benno Tallant swung the end of the blastick viciously. Even as the Kyban sank down nearly atop him, the looter felt a rugged thrill course down his veins; there was a pleasure he had never known in this sort of guerrilla warfare. From the first team-member he had taken the long, scythe-shaped knife with its inlaid tile handle.

It had worked wondrously well on the other four.

Kyban blood was yellow. He wasn't surprised.

By the time dawn slid glowingly up on the horizon, Tallant knew the Kyben were aware of his presence. What it meant, who he was, what he was doing on Deald's World . . . none of those answerables might have occurred to them as clearly as he phrased them, but thirty men had by that time died before the blue power of his blastick or the curve of his knife. And eventually they would be found where they lay; they would be reported missing; they would not check in.

Then the Kyban Command would know they were not alone on the planet.

All through the night he had heard robot patrol scouts circling overhead, trying to track down the neutrino emission of the bomb, and several times two or three had homed in on him. But at two miles radius they merely circled, waiting to pinpoint by ground search. But before the troops could close in, he had made good his escape, and they circled helplessly, waiting new instructions.

It seemed about the time for them to realize the bomb was in a moving carrier. What that carrier was, and the reason thirty troops were dead, would soon show themselves to be the same: a man alive on the planet.

The robot patrol scouts circled and buzzed overhead, and for a moment Tallant wondered how *they* had gotten aloft when a ship could not. Then he answered his question with the logical answer. The robots were just that—robots. Operating from mechanical means. The ships were inverspace ships, operating from warp-mechanisms. And it was obviously the warp pattern that set the bomb off.

So he could be easily tracked, but the Kyben could not leave, to chase and destroy the Earthies.

Tallant's fist balled and his dirt-streaked face twisted in a new kind of hatred as he thought of the men who had left him here to die. Parkhurst and Shep and Doc Budder and the rest. They who had left him here to this!

He was fooling them. He was staying alive!

*But wasn't that what they had wanted?* Hadn't they chosen properly? Wasn't he running to stay alive, allowing them to escape to warn Earth? What did he care for Earth? What had it ever given him?

He swore then, in a voiceless certainty deeper than mere frustration and anger, that he would more than survive. He would come out of this ahead. He wasn't sure *how* . . . but he would.

As the light of morning reached him through the jagged opening in the front of the building, where he lay on the floor, he vowed he would not die here on this—someone else's—battlefield.

He rose to his feet, and looked out through the blasted plasteel face of the building. The capital city of Deald's World stretched below him, and to the right.

In the center, towering higher than any building, was the command ship of the Kyban fleet.

Somehow, in the darkness, with the newly-acquired stealth of a Marsh animal, he had passed the outgoing Kyban troop lines, and was behind their front. He was inside the circle. Now he had to take advantage of that.

He sat down for a moment to think of his only way out.

Before the looting Kyban soldier stepped

into the room, he had arrived at the solution. He had to get to that Kyban ship, and get inside. He had to find a Kyban surgeon. It might be death, but it was a *might*; any other way it was a certainty.

He stood up to go, to skulk through the alleys of Xville to the ship, when the double-chinned, muscled Kyban came up the partially-ruined stairs, and stopped coldly in the entrance of the room, amazement mirrored on his puttied features. An Earthie . . . here on conquered ground!

He dragged his blastick from its sheath, aimed it, and fired dead-range at Tallant's stomach.

The shaft of blue light caught Tallant as he rocketed sideways. It seared at his flesh, and he felt an all-consuming wave of pain rip down through him. He had side-stepped partially, and the blast had taken him high on the right arm. He was horribly convulsed by agony for an instant, then . . .

He could not feel the right arm.

Tallant was moving as through a fog of pain, and in a moment, before the Kyban could fire again, had grabbed the blastick with his left hand. The little man felt a strange power coursing through him, and he dimly recognized it as the power of hatred; the hatred of all other men, all other beings, that had displaced his cowardice.

He ripped at the blastick violently, and

the alien was yanked toward him, thrown off-balance.

As the bewildered Kyban stumbled past, losing his hold on his own weapon, Tallant brought up a foot, and sent it slamming into the alien's back.

The yellow outworlder staggered forward, arms thrown out wildly, tripped over the rubble clogging the floor, and pitched headfirst through the rift in the wall.

Tallant limped to the hole and watched him fall, screaming.

"Aaaaaaaaaaaaaaaaaaarghhhhh!" and the sound of it whistled back up through the city's canyon, till it vanished with an audible thud thirty floors below. That scream, held and piercing, was more than a death knell. It was a signal. The area was a great sounding-board, and every foot of that screaming descent had been recorded on the walls and in the stones of the city.

The Kyben would be here shortly. Their comrade could not have driven them to their goal more effectively had he planned it.

Then Tallant realized something:

He had only one arm.

His eyes seemed to swing down without his willing them; he could feel no pain now; the blastick had cauterized the stump immediately. There would be no infection, there would be no more pain, but he was neatly amputated at the bicep. His eyes moved slightly and he gagged at the sight.

With one arm, what could he *hope* to accomplish?

How could he stay alive?

Then he heard the raised voices of the Kyben coming through the building; he knew they would investigate from where their comrade had fallen. He moved with wooden legs, feeling the fight draining out of him, but moving nonetheless.

Moving in a reflexive pattern of survival ... recognizing his only chance was to get to that Kyban flagship towering in the center of Xville. He had arrived at the lone chance, the final chance available to him, after close inspection of all paths out of this situation. That chance was almost certainly death, but the *almost* was a shade no other chance held.

His legs carried him out of the room, down a back flight of stairs, endlessly, endlessly down and somewhere along the way— probably in the room itself, but he could not quite remember—he carried the blastick. Then there was a time, as he wound down the interminable stairs, when he did *not* have the blastick. And even later, as he saw the big number 14 on the wall by the door, he had it again. As the numbers decreased, as 10 melted to 5 to 3, he realized he had come thirty flights ... entirely in shock.

When he was on the first floor, the front of the building was surrounded by Kyben, staring and motioning at the body of their comrade. Tallant looked away; he had thought himself inured to death, but the Kyban had died in a particularly unpleasant manner.

He shifted the blastick in the crook of his arm—the one arm left—and huddled back against the wall. There were three tortuous miles of ruined city and piled rubble between him and the flagship. (And once he was there, he had no assurance that the thing he sought would even be there!) Not to mention the entire land-army of the Kyban fleet, a horde of robot patrol scouts that must surely have realized the bomb was being carried by a man, and his own wounds.

He leaned the blastick against the wall, and felt gingerly at the stump of his arm. There was no pain, and the raw, torn end had been neatly, completely, like a bit of putty smoothed over, cauterized. He felt fine otherwise, though the night in the Blue Marshes had brought him a kink in the right leg, forcing him into an unconscious limp.

There was still a chance to make it.

At that moment he heard the public address system in the scout ship that circled the building. It boomed down, flooding the streets with sound; in English.

"EARTHMAN! WE KNOW YOU ARE HERE! GIVE YOURSELF UP BEFORE

66

YOU DIE! EVEN IF YOU CONTROL THE BOMB, WE WILL FIND YOU AND KILL YOU ... FIND YOU AND KILL YOU ... FIND YOU AND KILL YOU ..."

The robot scout ship moved off across the city, the same message over and over broadcast, till Tallant felt each word burning into his brain. *Find you and kill you, find you and kill you ...*

His breath came shortly, and he stumbled back against the wall, feeling its stony coolness under his hands. He closed his eyes, and drank deeply of emptiness. The path of cowardice was a twisting one. He had found that out. But though it might occasionally cross the road of bravery, it always passed back to the other path.

Tallant was frightened. He reached for his dream-dust.

Time was growing short, and Tallant could feel it in his gut.

He had no way of knowing whether the bomb was nearing triggering-time, but there was a vague, prickling sensation throughout his body that he interpreted as danger. The bomb might go off at any second, and that would be the end of it. Benno Tallant tightened his single fist into a painful ball; his rodent-like face drew down into an expression of blind fury, and the lines about his closed eyes grew deeper as he screwed his eyes tighter. He squeezed them till he heard a muted roaring in his ears; then he swore to himself he would come out ahead in this situation! Somehow, he knew no possible way it could come true, he was going to beat the lousy Earthies who had done this to him. He was going to get to that flagship . . . and when he did! He was going to win.

Not by cutting the corners the way a coward would . . . the way he had been doing it for years . . . but the way a winner does it, the way *he* was going to do it.

He hefted the blastick and turned to go.

The Kyben knew now that the bomb was in a human's hands. Not in a human's stomach—that they could *not* know—but in a human's hands. For their target had moved, shifted, eluded them all through the night. Obviously it was not buried or fastened down. Hidden in the best possible place . . . in a moving target. They were after him, and the net would be closing down. But there were a few things in his favor.

The most important of which was the fact that he had killed a number of patrolmen out in the fields, in the Marshes, and they would center their search in that area. They would not realize he had come through the sewer system into the capital city during the night.

He was safe for a while.

Even as Tallant thought that, as he moved toward the basement stairs of the ruined building, a Kyban officer, resplendent in sand-white uniform and gold braid, came through the door in front of him.

The man was unarmed, but in an instant he had whipped out the dress knife, and was making passes in the air before Tallant's face. That same feeling of urgency, of strength from some unknown pool within him, boiled up in Tallant. The officer was too close for Tallant to use the long blastick, but he still had the arc-shaped knife from the night before. He dropped the blastick softly into a pile of ash and slag-dust, ducked as the Kyban blade whistled past his ear, and leaped for the officer, before the other's hand could whip back around.

With his one hand fingers-out, Tallant reached the Kyban, drove the thin fingers deep into the man's eyes. The officer let out a piercing shriek as his eyeballs watered into pulp, and the prongs of Tallant's hand went into his head. Then, before the Kyban could open his mouth to shriek again, before he could do anything but wave his hands emptily in the air, feeling his eyes running down his cheeks, Benno Tallant drew his own scythe-shaped blade from his belt, and slashed the man's neck with one sidearm swipe.

The officer fell in a golden-blooded heap, and Tallant grabbed up his blastick, charging through the hall of the building, reaching the door that led to the basement, slamming it behind him, and plunging into the darkness of the building's depths.

Overhead he could hear the yells of Kyban foot-soldiers discovering their officer, but he didn't wait to have them discover him. Keeping careful track of which direction he faced, he felt around the floor of the basement till he contacted the sealplug that led to the sewers. He had come up through that polluted dankness the night before, seeking momentary rest, and fresh air.

He had climbed to the top of the building to see how the enemy was displaced, and fallen asleep—against his will. Now he was back to the sewers, and the sewers would carry him to the one lone chance for life he could imagine.

He ran his suddenly strong fingers around the edge of the sealing strip, and pried up the heavy lid with one hand.

He grimaced in the darkness. He *had* to pry it up with one hand . . . that was all they had left him.

Another moment and the port sighed up, counter-balanced, and Tallant slid himself over the lip, the blastick stuck through his belt. He kept himself wedged against the side of the hole, a few feet above the darkly swirling water of the sewer, and grabbed for the lid. The sealplug sighed down, and Tallant let himself drop.

The knife slid from his belt, fell into the water and was gone in an instant. He hit the tunnel wall as he fell, and came down heavily on one leg, tightening it, sending a pain shooting up through his left side.

He regained his footing by clawing at the slimy walls of the tunnel, and braced himself, legs widely apart against the dragging tide of the sewer water.

He kept pulling himself along the wall till he found a side-tunnel that headed in the proper direction. Just as he turned the corner, he saw the sealplug open, far back down the tunnel's length, and a searchbeam flooded the water with a round disc of light. They had suspected his means of escape already.

"Ssssisss sss sss kliss-isss!" He heard the sibilance of the Kyban speech being dragged down the hollowness of the tunnel to him. They were coming down into the sewers after him.

He had to hurry. The net was tightening. He knew he had a good chance of getting away, even though they had light and he had none.

They would have to try *all* the tunnels, but he would not; he would keep going in one direction, inexorably.

The direction that led to the gigantic Kyban flagship.

# VII

IT WAS A SHORT RUN FROM THE SEWER PLUG
that exited by the service entrance of what
had been a department store. A short run,
and he was hidden by the shadow of the
monstrous spaceship fin. A guard stood by
the ramp; guards stood at each ramp; Tallant circled.

He found a loading ramp, and the guard
slumped against the shining skin of the
deep-space ship. Tallant took a step toward
the man, realized he'd never make it in time.

The same strange urge to strike rose up
in Benno Tallant, showing him a way he
would not have considered the day before.
He could not use the blastick—too noisy; he
had lost the scythe-knife; he was too far

away to throw a boot and hope it would stun the guard.

So he walked out, facing the guard, coughing.

Carefully, nonchalantly, as though he had every right to be there. And as the guard heard the coughing, looked up, and amazedly watched Tallant stalking toward him ... Benno Tallant waved a greeting, and began to whistle.

The guard watched for a second.

The second was long enough.

Tallant had his hand around the man's neck before the guard could raise an alarm. One leg behind the Kyban's, and he was atop the guard. The butt of the blastick shattered the alien's flat-featured face, and the way was clear.

Tallant crouched as he walked up the ramp. Late morning light filtered across his back, and he held the cumbersome blastick with one hand on the trigger-stock, the weapon shoved under his armpit. He sprinted quickly up the ramp, slid his hand down the stock to the handle. The inside of the ship was cool and moist and dark.

Kyba was a cooler planet, and a moister planet, and a darker planet.

But all three congealed into a feeling of dank oppression that made Tallant wonder bleakly whether it was worth it; whether life was so important suddenly, that he should keep on moving, and not just lie down.

He saw what must have been a freight shaft, and stepped into it. There was no drag, and he pressed a button on the inner wall of the hollow tube. The suck was immediately generated, drawing him up through the ship.

He let himself slow by scraping his heels against the inner wall, at each layer of the ship, seeking the one escape factor he hoped was on board.

He saw no one. The ship's complement had been cut to the dregs, obviously. Every able-bodied man sent planetside to search for the bomb.

Here was the bomb ... walking through the mother ship.

Tallant began to sweat as he rose in the shaft; if he had figured incorrectly, if what he thought was aboard, was *not* aboard, he was doomed. He was ... he saw what he wanted!

The man was walking down a hall, directly in Tallant's line of sight as he peered from the freight tube. The man wore a long white smock, and though Tallant had no way of knowing for certain, he was sure the apparatus hanging about the man's neck was the equivalent of an electrostethoscope.

The Kyban was a doctor.

Tallant propelled himself from the shaft,

landed on the plasteel floor of the ship with legs spread, the blastick wedged between body and armpit, his hand tight to the trigger-stock.

The Kyban doctor stopped dead, staring at this man who had come from nowhere. The alien's eyes roved up and down Tallant's body, stopping for a long moment at the stump of the right arm.

Tallant moved toward the doctor, and the Kyban backed up warily. "English," Tallant asked roughly. "You speak English?"

The doctor stared silently at Tallant, and the Earthman squeezed a bit harder on the trigger-stock, till his knuckles went white with the strain of not blasting.

The Kyban doctor nodded simply. "There's got to be an operating room around here," Tallant went on, commandingly. "Take me there. Now!"

The doctor watched the man silently, till Tallant began to advance. Then he suddenly realized—for Tallant could see the dawning realization in the alien eyes—that the Earthie must need him for something, and would not—under *any* circumstances—shoot. Tallant saw the realization on the alien's flat-featured face, and a wild desperation struck up in him.

He backed the alien to the wall, and gripped the blastick farther down its length. Then he swung it, hard!

The muzzle cracked across the Kyban's

shoulder, and he let out a muted moan. Tallant hit him again, in the stomach; a third time across the face, opening a gash that ran to the temple. Had the Kyban not been nearly bald, his hair would have been matted with blood.

The alien sank back against the wall, began to slide down. Tallant kicked the man just below the double-jointed knee, straightening the doctor up.

"You'll stay alive, Doc . . . but don't try your stamina against mine. I've been up all night, running from your foot-soldiers. And right along now I'm getting pretty edgy. So you just walk ahead of me, and we'll see that operating room of yours."

The golden-skinned outworlder hesitated a fraction of a second, and Tallant brought his knee up with a snap. The medic screamed, then. High and piercing. Tallant knew the sound would carry through the ship, so he kicked out at the alien, driving him before the blastick.

"Now you get this straight, fella," Tallant snarled. "You're going to walk ahead of me, right straight to that operating room, and you're going to do a little surgery on me . . . and one move, so help me God, *one move* that seems unlikely, and I take off the top of your yellow skull. Now *move it!*"

He jabbed the blastick hard into the Kyban's back, and the medic tottered off down the hall.

They were passing a utility rack—loaded with leg chains and head braces and manacles, used by the Kyben to keep prisoners in tow—when the Kyban sergeant struck. He had heard the scream, come out of the wardroom, and positioned himself in the alcove behind the utility rack, waiting for Tallant and the doctor to come his way. The attack was too hurried, however; and as the sergeant lunged for Tallant and, wrenched the blastick from his hands to ensure the medic's safety, Tallant whirled away, and smashed the glass of the utility rack.

In a moment his reflexes had taken over, and he bore no slightest resemblance to the quivering Benno Tallant who had cried to Parkhurst for his life. Now he was an avenging devil. His hand closed about a long, heavy-link leg chain, and brought it whistling free from its pincers and through the air with a snap.

The chain caught the Kyban sergeant along the base of the skull, and the man choked out a sibilant nothing as his brain was smashed in its case.

He fell frontwards, crashing against the medic who had been reaching for the dropped blastick, and they tumbled to the plasteel floor together.

The chain was imbedded in the Kyban's head.

Tallant took a short step and brought his booted foot down with a crunch on the medic's hand. Hard enough to discourage the alien's reaching . . . but not hard enough to impair his surgical ability.

Tallant spotted a service revolver halfway drawn from its snugger on the Kyban sergeant's belt, and he drew the sleek little sliver-nosed pistol, pointing it at the medic.

"This is better.

"Let's go."

The medic got to his feet with difficulty, groaning as he rose. He knew now that Tallant was more dangerous than an entire army. The Earthman was desperate, really desperate, and he knew why: this must be the one who had the bomb. The Commandant had been talking about this man the night before, when they had realized a man was still alive on Deald's World.

He had taken a great deal of punishment, and he knew the Earthie would continue to deal it out; not enough to kill him, but the pain would be very great.

The Kyban doctor was no hero.

The operating room was inevitable.

"And take your comrade with you," Tallant added.

The medic grabbed up the sergeant's feet and dragged him behind as he walked toward the operating room. The trail of blood was faintly golden against the plasteel floor plates. Tallant kicked the blastick into the alcove. They might not come down through this corridor too soon, still looking as they were for him, outside the city.

The operating room was inevitable.

Tallant refused to take even a local anesthetic. He sat propped up on the operating table, the sliver-shaft revolver pointed directly at the medic. The Kyban stared at the cylinder of the gun, saw the little capsules in their chambers, thought of how they were fired through the altering mechanism, how they came out as raw energy, and he wielded the electroscalpel with care.

Tallant's face became beaded with sweat as the incisions were made; though he hardly felt the electric beam cut through the flesh. But as the layers of flesh that had been the scar peeled back, and he again saw his innards, wet and pulsing, he remembered the first time.

Things had changed, *he* had changed since Doc Budder had put the bomb in his belly. Now he was nearing the end of the path . . . starting a new one.

In twenty minutes it was over.

Tallant had guessed correctly.

The bomb could *not* be set off under cautious operating conditions. Parkhurst had made great mention of the inverspace drive's warp field setting it off, and of the bomb detonating of its own accord when the time came. But when it had come to mention of the Kyben removing it, he had threatened Tallant only with being cut to ribbons. Perhaps it had been Parkhurst's subconscious way of offering Tallant a chance; perhaps it had just been an over-sight in the Resistance leader's explanation ... but in either case, the operation had been completed successfully, and the bomb was out.

Tallant watched carefully as the Kyban put an alien version of an epidermizer on the wound. He watched steadily for a half hour as the scar built up.

Then he was whole again, and the danger had been extracted from his belly.

He stared at the medic carefully, said in level tones:

"Graft the bomb to my stump."

The medic's dark eyes opened wider; he blinked rapidly, and Tallant repeated what he had said. The medic backed away, know-ing what purpose Tallant had in mind—or *thinking* he knew, which was the same thing as far as Tallant was concerned.

It took ten minutes of pistol-whipping for Tallant to realize the medic would go only so far, and no farther. The physician would *not* graft the total destruction sun-bomb to the stump of Tallant's right arm.

... at least ... not under his own will.

The idea dawned slowly, but when formed was clear and whole and practica-ble. Tallant reached into his jumper pocket, extracted one of the last two packets of dream-dust. He bent down, and under pressure, made the half-conscious Kyban sniff it. He got the entire packet, the full, demolishing dose into the alien's nostrils. Then he settled back to wait, remembering the first time he had met the dream-dust.

The memory flooded back, and he recalled that the first, imprudent whiffing had made him a confirmed addict; it was powerful that way.

When the medic awoke, he would be an addict ... would do *anything* for that last packet nestling in Tallant's jumper pocket.

The Earthman knew he would never again be God—or at least till he could locate more dust—but it was worth it, for what he had in mind. *More* than worth it.

He waited, knowing they would not be disturbed. The Kyben were out looking for him, and the emissions of the ship around him would confuse the robot scouts; he was safe for the time being. And when the medic awoke, he would do *anything* Tallant wanted.

Tallant wanted only one thing.

The sun-bomb grafted to his arm, where he could detonate it in an instant.

There had been no pain. The same force that had ripped Tallant's arm to atoms, had deadened the nerve ends. The bomb was set into the flesh slightly, a block at the end of the stump. With a simple wire hookup that would detonate under several circumstances:

If Tallant consciously triggered the bomb.

If anyone tried to remove the bomb against his will.

If he died, and his heart stopped.

The Kyban doctor had done his work well. Now he huddled, shaking under the effects of total dust addiction, moaningly begging Tallant for the last packet.

"Sure, mister, you can have the snuff." He held the clear plastic packet between two fingers, so the Kyban could see both the revolver and the dust at once. "But first, first. First you take me updecks to meet your Commandant."

The Kyban's eyes were golden slits, but they widened now as he tried to comprehend what the Earthie meant. He had thought he knew what the man was after . . . to get rid of the bomb and leave Deald's World. But now . . .

He was confused, terrified. What was this insatiable hunger that clawed at him, and made his every nerve a burning wire? The Earthman had done it to him, and somehow, he knew that little white packet held the end of his hunger.

He hardly realized he had led the Earthman to the bridge, but when he looked again, they were there, and the Commandant was staring wide-eyed at them, demanding an explanation. Needing none, really.

Then, as the doctor watched, Tallant raised the revolver and fired. The shot took away half the Commandant's face, and he spun sidewise, spraying himself across the port. The body tumbled to the floor and rolled a few inches, to the edge of the drop-shaft. Tallant walked past the doctor, and calmly nudged the body over with his boot. The body hung there a split instant, then dropped out of sight as a stone down a well.

There was only one more step to take.

Tallant walked over to the doctor, examining him carefully as he came nearer. The man was a typical Kyban . . . a bit shorter than most, with a protruding stomach, and a head that would be quite bald in a few years.

His skin was the aging off-gold of the Kyban race, and his face was strong. Strong, that is (Tallant noted), with the exception of the infinitesimal tic in the cheek and lower lip, the hunger lines about the mouth and eyes. The good doctor was now an addict, and that suited Tallant just fine.

He found a weird pleasure in having bent this man so simply to his design. He found the events of the past day invigorating, now that they were over.

And as the face of the doctor grew larger in his eyes, Benno Tallant took stock of himself. The bad in him—and he was the first to admit it was there, festering deeper than any superficial nastiness—had not changed one bit. It had not become good, it had not tempered him into mellow thoughts through his trials, it had left him only harder. It had matured itself.

For years, as he skulked and begged, as he weaseled and cheated, his strength of evil had been going through an adolescence. Now it was mature. Now he had direction, and he had purpose. Now he was no longer a coward, for he had faced all the death the world could throw at him, and had bested it. He had outsmarted the Earthmen, he had outmaneuvered the Kyban. He had bested the foot-soldiers in the field, and the mathematicians in the bunkers. He had lived through the bomb, and the attack of the aliens, and the night of terror and all it held otherwise. He had come through the Marshes, and the fields, and the city, to this final place.

To this cabin of the fleet ship.

But he was not the Benno Tallant the Earthmen had found the day before, looting a dead shopkeeper. He was another man entirely. A man whose life had taken the one possible turn it could ... for the other turn—*death*—was a stranger to him.

Benno Tallant shoved the doctor ahead of him, to the banks of controls.

He paused, turning the shaking addict to him. He stared into the golden slits, and the golden face, and realized with consummate pleasure that he did not hate these men who had tried to find him and cut out his belly; he admired them, for they were engaged in taking what they wanted.

No, he didn't hate *them*.

"What is your name, my good old friend?" he asked cheerily.

The doctor's hand, tentacle-ended, came up quivering, to beg for the last packet. Tallant slapped the hand away; he did not hate the aliens, but he had no room for sympathy. All that of decency and compassion was gone—burned away by the blast of hell in the bombed-out building, eaten away by the cruelty of his fellow Earthmen. He was hard now, and reveled in it.

"Your name!"

The doctor's tongue quivered over the word: "Norghese."

"Well, Doctor Norghese, you and I are going to be ever such good friends, you know that? You and I are going to do big things together, aren't we?"

In the quivering, chill-raked body of the little doctor, Tallant knew he had a slave from this time on. He clapped the alien about the shoulders.

"Find me the communications rig in this mess, Doc."

The alien pointed it out, and on command, threw the switch that connected Tallant to the men in the field, to the ships that were settled all across Deald's World, to the skeleton crew of the ship in which he stood.

He lifted the speak-stick, and stared at it for a moment. He had considered blowing up the fleet, ordering it to return home, a number of things.

But that had been the day before when he had been Tallant the Trembling.

This was today.

And he was a new Benno Tallant.

He spoke sharply and shortly.

"This is the last man on Deald's World, my Kyban friends. I'm the man your superiors have finally realized carried the sun-bomb.

"Hear me now!

"I *still* carry it. But now I control it. I can set it off at any moment, and kill us all . . . even in space. For the power of this bomb is incalculable. If you doubt me, I will let you speak to Doctor Norghese of the mother ship, in a few moments, and he will verify what I've said.

"But you have no reason to fear, for I'm going to offer you a deal far superior to anything you had as mere Kyban soldiers on conquest missions for your home world.

"I offer you the chance to become conquerors in your own right. Now that you've been away from home for years, and are weary of battle, I'll offer you the chance to come home not just as tin heroes, but as

87

warriors with money and worlds at your command.

"Does it matter to you who leads this fleet? As long as you conquer the galaxies? I don't think it does!"

He paused, knowing they would see it his way. They would have to see it that way. Planetary allegiance only went so far, and he could turn this home-hungry planetful of foot-soldiers into the greatest conquering force ever born.

"Our first destination is ..." he paused, knowing he was hewing a destiny he could never escape, "... Earth!"

He handed the speak-stick to the doctor, shoved him once to indicate he wanted verification of what he had said, listened for a moment to make sure the doctor's sibilant monotone in English was appropriate.

Then he walked to the viewport, and stared out as the dusk fell again across the city of Xville, and the fields of slowly-ripening Summerset, and beyond them the Marshes and the Faraway Mountains.

He watched it all ... Deald's World ... and made a vow that his revenge would be long and detailed.

Then something Parkhurst had said, oddly enough, leaped to mind as appropriate for this time and this place and his new life:

*I don't hate you. But this has to be done.*

*It has to be done, and you will have to do it. But I don't hate you.*

He thought the thoughts, and knew they were true.

He didn't hate anyone now. He was above that; he was Benno Tallant, and now there was no need for the dust; he was cured.

He turned away from the port and looked about at the ship that would mold his destiny, knowing he was free of Deald's World, free of the dust. He needed neither now.

Now he was God on his own.

# Echoes of Thunder

```
/__|
0000    STRANGER, JOHN
0001    TRANS-UNITED RESERVATION D5-SOUTH DAKOTA-116
0002    SOC 187735-NN-000
0003    4 APR 2177—1:46 PM
0004
0005    IMMEDIATE REPLY MANDATORY BY LAW
0006    REFER TRANS-UNITED DIRECTIVE 2045 E, SECTION 12
0007    REFER TRIBAL TREATY SUNDOWN
0008
0009    GREETINGS JOHN STRANGER
0010    FROM THE TRANS-UNITED SPACE ENGINEERING CORP
0011
0012    CONGRATULATIONS UPON BEING SELECTED BY T.U.S.E.
0013    FOR ORIENTATION AND TRAINING ON STATION CENTRAL
0014
```

```
0015    YOU WILL REPORT TO YOUR TERMINAL INDUCTION BLDG
0016    ON 7 APR 2177—6:00 PM
0017
0018    DO NOT BRING TOILET ARTICLES OR A CHANGE OF CLOTHES
0019    ALL WILL BE PROVIDED
0020
0021    WELCOME ABOARD
0022    FROM YOUR TRANS-UNITED DRAFT COUNCIL
0023
0024    YOUR PRESENCE IS REQUIRED BY LAW
0025    YOUR PRESENCE IS REQUIRED BY TRIBAL TREATY
0026
0027    REFER USCC DIRECTIVE 27AI INDIGENOUS PEOPLES
0028
0029    /*ROUTE PRINT REMOTE 2
0030    /*ROUTE PRINT LOCAL 7
0030    1234567890123456
0031/*
END     SOC I87735FILE-NN-000
```

The old man walked beside John Stranger, staring down at the rocky trail. It was not a time to talk. His face was leather, as wrinkled as the earth. His lips were chapped and parched, as if they had never touched water. Years beyond counting had marked him, molded him. Now he was age-less, timeless.

The stark landscape stretched out below them: muddy columns carved by wind, deep ravines, vertical dikes, fluted ridges. It was desolate country. But it was their country. The way down would be difficult, but Broken-finger could climb almost as well as John. He often boasted that the Great Spirit would not make him weak and sick before taking him "south"—the direction of death. He had always been strong. He was an Indian, not a *wasicun*, not a white man. He would take his strength with him to the outer world of the dead. That was his belief. That was his reality. It had always served him well.

Broken-finger was a medicine man. Since John Stranger was a child, the old man had taught him, trained him. That would all change.

They climbed down a sharp basalt cliff face, carefully searching out toeholds and handholds. Their progress was slow, the sun baked them unmercifully. But they were used to it; it was part of their lives. When they reached a rocky shelf about halfway down the cliff face, they paused to rest.

"Here," Broken-finger said, handing John a thermos of bitter water. "We can wait while you regain your strength."

John felt dizzy again. Had it really been

four days since he had climbed alone into the vision pit? Time had blurred, scattered like sand before the wind.

"You had a good vision," Broken-finger said. It was not a question, but a statement. He knew. It required no answer.

John blinked, focused his eyes. The spirit-veils were fluttering before him, shaking up the yellow grass and rocks and hills below like rising heat. He could see his village in the distance, nestled between an expansive rise and the gently rounded hills beyond. It had been his home since birth. Seventeen years had passed. It seemed like more. At times, it seemed like less.

The village was comprised of fifty silvery hutches set in a great circle, in the Indian way. Broken-finger used to say that a square could not have much power. But a circle is a natural power; it is the design of the world and the universe. The square is the house and risor of the wasicun, the squared-off, divided-up, vertical white man.

"Everyone down there is waiting for you," Broken-finger said, as if reading John's thoughts. "A good sweat lodge has been prepared to sear your lungs and lighten your heart. Then there will be a celebration."

"Why a celebration?" John asked, as he watched a spotted eagle soaring in circles against the sharp blue sky. It was brother to the eagle in his vision. Perhaps the spirit-man was watching.

"The village is making you a good-time because you must make a difficult decision. Pray your vision will help you."

"What has happened?" John stoppered the thermos, passed it back to the old man.

"We received news from the wasicun corporation yesterday." He paused, saddened, and stared straight ahead. "They claim their rights on you."

John Stranger felt a chill crawl down his back. He stood up and walked to the edge of the shelf; there he raised his hands and offered a prayer. He looked for the spotted eagle and, as if in a vision, imagined that it was flying away from him like an arrow through the clouds.

"We must go now," he said to Broken-finger, but he felt afraid and alone, as if he were back in the vision pit. He felt hollowed-out inside, as isolated as a city-dweller. They climbed down toward the village together; but John was alone, alone with the afterimages of his vision and the dark smoke of his thoughts and fears.

Below him, the village caught the sun and seemed to be bathed in spirit-light.

*

With an easy fluid motion John un-snapped the end of his tether and moved to the next position on the huge beam. His feet automatically found the hold-tight indentations at the adjacent work station. For a brief moment his body hung free of any support. He was weightless and enjoyed the feeling of freedom. This was one of the few pleasures up here to his liking. Earth hung above his head: a mottled globe, half darkness, half light. The cross-strut he needed floated slowly toward him. Anna was right behind it. Of all the damn luck—Anna. Anybody else. He shifted the joiner to his right hand and attached the proper nipple. There were twenty other floaters out on this shift; they could have sent someone else. The chatter on the intercom bothered him. He tongued down the gain.

"Bellman to Catpaw Five." The direct communication cut through the static and low-tone babble. Mike Elliot was bellman; John was Catpaw Five. The bellman directed the placing of the beams, the floaters did the work.

"Five here," slurred John. Mike was a stickler for rules and regulations. From the deck he could afford to be. It was different outside.

"Strut alpha omega seven-one-four on its way."

"I have eyes," said John.

"Acknowledge transmission, Catpaw Five." Always by the book.

"Transmission acknowledged. Visual confirmation of alpha omega seven-one-four has been achieved. Satisfied?"

"This transmission is being monitored, Catpaw Five."

"They're all monitored, so what's the difference? Fire me."

"I wish I could."

"I wish you would." Damn uppity bellman. They were all the same. "And while you're at it, why did you send Grass-likelight? She has second shift today."

"She goes by Anna, floater, and I put her out because I wanted to."

"You put her out because she's a royal pain in my—"

"You're on report, John."

"Stuff it."

"Firing on five. Mark."

The seconds ticked down in his head. It was automatic—and he had already forgotten Mike. At the count of zero, three low-grade sparklers fired. Aluminum trioxide, mined on the Moon. These one-time rockets were cheap and dirty, but all they needed. The boron filament beam, its apparent movement stopped, hovered a meter to his left. Sloppy.

"You missed," John said.

"You're still on report."

John shook his head, reached out with the grapple and pulled the near end toward the join. Mike was always excited, always putting floaters on report. It didn't mean a thing. People were cheap, but the ability to walk high steel wasn't common. They could hire and fire ten bellmen before they would touch a floater. Anyone could work the calculations, but walking the steel was a rare talent. There was no way he could ignore Anna.

"Down," he said, activating the local channel.

Anna fixed a firing ring around the far end of the beam and slowly worked it into position. She drifted easily, lazily. The beam slid gracefully into plumb.

"That's got it," he said. "Thanks," he added as an afterthought.

"You're welcome," she said in a dry voice. Without another word, she hit her body thrusters and moved away from him to her next position.

John ignored the snub and went to work with the joiner. Five of the color-coded joints were within easy reach; he didn't even have to move from the hold-tights. Some ground-based jockey had probably figured it all out before the plans were shipped up and the beams forged in space. As usual, they had blown the obvious cross-joins. He had to unhook for those, swing his body around to the other side. What looked easy on paper was often a different matter in space. His helmet lamp created a glare in his eyes as it reflected off the beam. The blind-side joins were the worst—no support. He clipped his joiner back on his belt and took a breather.

100

The tube that connected the globes of the barbell was taking shape. He'd been on the job for almost a month, from the very beginning. The tube looked like a skeleton now, but soon the outer skin would be worked into place and this job would be finished. After that, it was on to the next assignment. He could see several other floaters working on the tube—anonymous white-suited figures in the distance.

"That's got it, shift one," came the bellman's voice over the intercom. "Come on in."

John waited for the transport, really nothing more than a raft drifting by. It had been an uneventful shift; most of them were. They were ahead of schedule. That, too, was normal. Damn Anna, anyway. Damn Mike for slipping her on his shift. He knew how much that bothered him. John was used to his regular crew, knew their habits and eccentricities by heart. He didn't need other people. He didn't need Anna.

When the transport drifted by, he reached out and hooked himself on by the grapple. It was showy, but he didn't care. He looked to see if Anna noticed. She didn't seem to.

It didn't matter, he told himself.

*

"The skids are arriving right on schedule," Anna said, pointing at the nearest port. Outside, the small crafts blinked and glittered against the darkness. John

Stranger didn't look; he made a point of not turning his head. It was loud in the ward room, too many people packed into too small a place. After the riggers left, they would put up partitions, make it comfortable for the small number of people who would man the manufacturing station. Now they were packed in like fish in a tin. Riggers got little respect and fewer comforts. She leaned toward him across the small table, and it made him uncomfortable, although it didn't mean anything. Everyone leaned forward while resting in zero-g. It was reflex. A pencil floated past her face.

"So go have a good time," John said. The independent whores, male and female, always arrived just before the topping-off party. They were direct competition to the T.U.S.E.-supplied whores, who were more expensive but classier. It was almost time for the party. The job was almost finished. Soon the flag would be secured. Then would come the release, the time for the crew to become as blind and as drunk for as long as possible at the Bosses' expense.

"What I do is my business," Anna said. "As it happens, I plan to have a good time. That is still permitted."

John twisted his foot compulsively into the hold-tight grid on the floor. "You've turned white enough. Go ahead and have a good time with the wasicun."

"I'm not white," she said defensively,

pulling away from him. Only the hold-tights prevented her from floating to the ceiling. "You're a hypocrite," she said bitterly. "You're no more Indian than the rest of your friends." She waved her arm at the others in the room. "Some medicine man. Are *these* your people?"

John's face burned with anger and embarrassment. "Yes," he said. He was to have been a *wichasha waken*, a holy man, a healer. Clearly half the riggers—the floaters—were his own, his own blood. They were Indian, yet they weren't. They had turned away from their heritage, forgotten the way of the Sacred Pipe. They had jumped at the chance of reward, of a path out of the restrictive life of the ever-dwindling reservations. He could not understand, nor could he forgive. He had been taken away from his people, while most of them had left to become white men. A few, it was true, had been drafted. Anna was one.

She grinned at John, as if she could see right into him. "Spend the night with me," she said, baiting him. "Or aren't you man enough?"

"Our ways are not the same."

"Up here we are all the same," she said. "We are no longer in the woods, we are no longer dirtwalkers." She unlocked her cleats from the grid. Before pushing off she said, "John Stranger, I think you're impotent. I don't think you could even do it with a wasicun."

John winced. Perhaps he had studied the ways of the People too long and didn't know enough about the world. But the People were the world!

The lights flashed twice, a signal. Fred Ransome, one of the bosses, walked through the ward room shouting, "All right, riggers. Playtime's over. Now move. Get yourselves back into the dark."

John rose, cleared his head. He was pulling a double shift, like most of the other floaters. He didn't mind the work, just the people he worked for. While he was working, he could forget—forget that he was outside the sacred circle, forget Anna's face and her words.

He would not take Anna, nor any of the whores. He was a *wichasha waken*, a medicine man, even here. He was. *He was!* They could not take that away from him, no matter where they moved him, no matter what they made him do.

But in his heart, he was not so sure.

\*

The shifts seemed to blur, one melting into another, as constant and predictable as the stars. Somehow immense loads of planking moved into place. Endless floating mountains of beams were connected into struts and decking. Slowly the skeleton grew, took shape. The two massive globes at opposing ends of the station were each large enough to house a fair-sized city. They dwarfed the tube that connected them, even though the tube itself was over fifty meters in diameter. Pipes, endless mazes of twisted wires, and interlocking tunnels ran through the length of the tubes. Waldos walked down large tracks where the men would not be able to stand the gravity. In the middle of the connecting tube was a smaller globe, ringed with ports. It would hold the personnel manning the station.

Now the silvery covering was in place, and what had once looked as light as a delicate mobile seemed to gain in mass as strut after strut had been overlaid with the metallic skin.

Like predators circling a great whale, the tiny skids and larger T.U.S.E. ships floated, patient as the coming and going of the seasons. Even from where he stood at the aft end of the barbell, John could make out the details of the jury-rigged skids, odd pieces of junk bought or stolen, thrown together almost casually. The skids were dangerous, the reason for the high mortality rate of the freebooters. But they were free; free to die, work, or skiff off toward the asteroids, there to mine and get by until caught.

The freebooters were the people who had slipped through the otherwise smoothly running cogs of life in space. They belonged to no nation-state, no corporation, no colony. They came and went as they pleased selling services and paying for what they needed, stealing if they could not pay. They were rarely bothered by the officials—in this area the T.U.S.E. Patrol—as long as they maintained a low profile. Over a hundred thousand people lived and worked in space, and the freebooters were an insignificant percentage. They moved easily, usually unseen, from the richest condo to the roughest manufacturing complex. If they made waves, they were dealt with, usually by dumping them out into space. Without a suit.

The skids held pleasures of a coarse and vulgar nature. The T.U.S.E. corporation men on site made much use of them, the illegality of the situation adding greatly to the excitement. The freebooters were one of the darker sides of life in space.

But their lives were free.

The rest of the crew caught up with John. He clipped himself to Sam Woquini, and they started to crab their way across the silvery skin of this dormant creature they had helped create. They worked as one, easily, as they had for the last year, without giving danger a thought, for their interdependence was mutual.

The Boss had ordered this final walkthrough. As usual, he had wanted it done immediately. Everything had to be rushed. They had finished three weeks ahead of schedule and still the Boss hadn't let up. John tried not to let it bother him; it was just the city-dweller mentality, the wasicun way of life. They had yet to learn patience, to learn how to flow easily with the life forces.

All across the station the floaters drifted, making their final visual check. It was largely unnecessary, but protocol required it. They were dwarfed by the gargantuan structure they had given birth to, small specks against their grandiose creation.

John let his mind wander as he and Sam made their lazy way across the surface. He recognized the small signs of his own work as well as those of others. It was strangely comforting. There was pride involved here, satisfaction at a job well done. That was one of the few rewards of his situation. It could almost make up for the static he caught from the Bosses—T.U.S.E. brass—clowns, every one of them. It could never make up for the time they'd stolen from him, the years lost, away from the ways of his people. He felt the bitterness rise. He felt cheated.

\*

The geodesic had docked and the party had been in full swing for over an hour. John had no intention of going. He sat with Sam on a large skid that had been used to haul material around during the construction of the station. Since the job was, for all practical purposes, finished, it had been moved well away from the station. A large collection of equipment hung in space around them, ready to be moved to the next job.

"Stranger and Woquini, get your respective butts over here. Time to make an appearance." Mike Elliot's voice came through scratchy and loud on the voice box inside John's helmet. Elliot, the bellman, always seemed to be shouting. He knew the floaters kept their volume controls at the lowest setting.

"We're not going to make an appearance," John said. Wasicun always have to make noise, he thought. Only Sam knows how to be quiet.

"You're coming, and right now," shouted Elliot. "There's brass over here that wants to meet you. If you no-show, it's an automatic extension at my option. You know the rules. Right now I'm of a mind to tack a few years on. Might teach you a lesson."

That was always the kicker. They had draftees by the short hairs and could extend their tour for nearly any reason at all. When the corporations had worked out the conscription agreement with the government, they had held all the power, all the cards. Most of the land, too.

"I can make things hard for your friend." Elliot was getting frantic. His voice cracked. Must be getting a lot of pressure.

John would have stalled on general princi-
ples, but there was Sam.

"Don't do it on my account," said his
friend. "How hard can they make it for me?
I've got a contract."

John knew about contracts; they were no
better than the treaties of the past. They
could be bent, broken, twisted in a thousand ways. He shook his head.

"We'd better go," he said. He looked at
the Earth below him. The horizon seemed
to be made of rainbows. It shifted as he
watched. An erupting volcano traced a lazy
finger of smoke. He'd been watching it for
a month. A storm, one of the great ones,
twisted and flickered in the ocean. All this
beauty, and he had to go into a crowded
geodesic and make small talk with the
T.U.S.E. brass, fat cats that had never been
alone a moment in their lives and were
driven to turn Earth and space into frogskin dollars.

There was a small cycle tethered to a
docking adapter on the skid. John moved
toward it. "Give me a hand," he said to Sam,
and they swung the cobbled-up cycle into
position.

The cycle was the usual floater variety,
simple, made out of parts lying around. It
was just a collection of spare struts joined
together and a tiny thruster that powered
it with bursts of nitrogen. Several other cycles of similar design were scattered

around the construction site. Floaters used them to get wherever they were going and left them there for the next person.

John gripped one of the struts and aimed the thruster. "Hop on," he said to Sam.

"No, thanks," he said. "I'm going the fun way."

Sam grabbed a whipper and swung it over his head, catching it on the edge of the skid with a perfect motion that was a combination of long practice and an innate skill that could never be taught. He let it pull his body up in an arc and let loose of the whipper at the precise moment that would allow his angular momentum to carry him to the geodesic docked at one of the swollen ends of the manufacturing station. His body spun end over end with a beautiful symmetrical motion. He let out a loud whoop that rattled John's voice box even with the volume turned all the way down. John smiled at his friend, then laughed. Sometimes Sam did crazy things just for the fun of it. On the reservation he would have become an upside-down man, a joker, the holy trickster. Up here he had respect: he was very large and good with his hands, sometimes with his fists. Sam's whoop rose and fell. It was full of joy, the joy of living.

"Clear all channels," shouted Elliot. "What is that? Who's in trouble? Stranger, is Woquini okay? It sounds like he's dying."

"He's not dying," said John. "He's liv-

110

ing." He doubted Elliot would know the difference. He squeezed the thruster and headed for the geodesic.

*

The T.U.S.E. geodesic globe was actually a pleasure station brought in for the topping-off party. It was expensive, but the corporation could well afford it. There was enough gambling, sex, and cheap thrills available to satisfy all but the most jaded palates.

Sleds, flitters, skids, and cycles clustered all around the end of the barbell-shaped station and the docked geodesic. Parties like this brought the whores and hucksters out in force, along with the independents looking for work, hoping to sign on with someone. Independents were always looking for work, existence was precarious without corporate patronage. There were even private cabs—small energy-squandering vehicles—bearing the insignia of other corporations. They had come to check out the competition, look over the terrain, make connections, wheel and deal.

Off in the distance solar collectors hung in silent, glittering beauty for kilometers and kilometers. To John, they were a bead game in space, mirrors for Earth. They were beautiful, they were useful. They were in balance. The image of a bird in flight, somehow frozen, came to John. It was perfect—harmony and balance. How could such things be made by the wasicun? All this for the frogskin.

John and Sam arrived simultaneously at the entrance to the geodesic. Sam's trajectory, which would have given a computer a headache, was perfect. They had both known it would be. They unsuited and allowed themselves to be dragged into the party.

The topping-off party was a tradition that went back hundreds of years, its origin lost in legend and fable. At completion of work on a project—be it bridge, barn, or skyscraper—a flag, or sometimes a tree, was placed on the highest part of the structure. It was a christening of sorts and accompanied by a party, nearly always at the company's expense. If the owners declined to supply the whiskey for the party, the flag was replaced by a broom, expressing the workers' displeasure and embarrassing the company.

Like much of man's life on Earth, this tradition was carried into space. It was never planned, it just happened. It gave the men roots, a sense of place. For the same reason, the person who directed the placing of the beams was called a bellman, though bells hadn't been used as a signal in hundreds of years.

It was loud in the geodesic, much too loud for John. A mixture of floaters and corporation brass milled around, along with a

scattering of other hangers-on, independents, whores. The corporation brass were
easy to pick out by their obvious inability
to handle zero-g. He picked out the floaters,
equally obvious by their advanced stages of
intoxication. They were a mixed ethnic bag:
Scandinavians, Germans, Irish, Scots, His-
panics, the ever-present English. Most of
them, however, were his own people, in
blood if not in thought. As usual, they were
making fools of themselves before the white
man. He fought a rush of hatred, not only
for the wasicun, but for his own people as
well.

He was immediately ashamed, for in his
heart he felt he was no different than the
others. He found his oblivion in his work,
his dreams, his love of the immensities of
space. They found their oblivion in booze,
sex, and drugs. He was a freak, the outcast,
not they.

The only other person he had met up here
that came close to holding to the ways of
the People was Sam. But Sam had chosen
space; he had not been drafted. He seemed
to have struck a balance between the old
life and the new. In a way, John envied him.

He sometimes thought he saw some of the
signs of the old life in Anna, though they
were deeply buried. He got the feeling that
she had turned her back on her past. John
was a constant reminder of those times to

her. Perhaps, he thought, that was why they never got along.

A young woman drifted over to John, offered him a nipple of scrag. He politely refused—it would be a double bind if he was high and anything happened. Most of the floaters could handle it, but he knew he couldn't. He would be leaving the party as soon as possible.

A well-dressed man in his late sixties was holding court with a man about half his age. The younger man was a dirtwalker by all appearances. He stood perfectly still as if one wrong move would send him floating away forever. His legs were tense, his feet jammed firmly in the hold-tights on the floor grid. His knees were locked. It would take a collision with a skimmer running full bore to dislodge him. Uncomfortable as he looked, he was hanging on every word.

"Great return," said the older man. "Great return. You just can't beat space for high-percentage income.

John shook his head, pushed away. He'd heard that conversation a thousand times, was sick to death of it. If they dragged him into their talk, he'd say something wrong and get into trouble for sure.

There was new gossip from the belt, chatter about business interests on the Moon, but mostly talk centered around the station they'd just finished. Everyone seemed to think it was a marvelous feat of engineering. When set into rotation, the station would produce a graduated gravity source, with a maximum of fifty-g's at the rounded ends. It could never have been achieved on Earth. What would eventually be manufactured there was a mystery to John—more square cities for all he knew or cared. It was a job, plain and simple. He was pleased that the floaters' end had worked out well; beyond that he had very little interest.

Two of the T.U.S.E. brass separated from a crowd and kicked over toward him. There was no easy way to escape. He braced himself.

"So you're John Stranger," said one of them. "I understand you're one of our best men up here."

"Do you know me?" he asked, making an attempt to be civil.

The man smiled and tapped his ear, indicating that he wore a computer plug. He turned to his companion.

"Mr. Stranger here is an American Indian, as many of our floaters are. They work well on the beams, seem to have no fear at all. We recruit and draft heavily from the tribes. They seem to have natural ability in their blood. Wouldn't you say that was true, Mr. Stranger?" He took a sniffer from his pocket, inhaled deeply. Some sort of drug, a stimulant, most likely.

John was insulted. People made the most sweeping generalizations. He swallowed his anger. It would serve no purpose to start trouble with the brass. He'd spend the rest of his life in servitude that way.

"Some say that," said John, instantly sorry he'd compromised himself. A cowardly action. "I'd better get back into the dark," he added, moving away. The man caught his arm.

"Can't leave now," he said. "This party's for you, for all of you. Can't thank you enough. You men and women are the real backbone of our operation."

The thought turned John's stomach. "I really have to be going," he said. If he didn't get out, he was going to do something foolish. He almost didn't care.

"We're having a spin party later in the living quarters on the station when they start the rotation. Just a few of us old boys and some selected friends. Ought to be pretty spectacular. If you're free, consider yourself invited."

"I'll keep it in mind," said John, swallowing his contempt, backing off. No way he'd show up at something like that.

Breaking away from the two men, he caught a glimpse of Anna across the room. She was talking with a young man, a pretty whore. She met his stare arrogantly, as if they were two opposing forces, two incompatible states of mind. She turned her attention back to the boy.

John was depressed. There were things about Anna that he felt drawn to, others that forced him away. It was a complex feeling. It was unsettling.

He had to get out of the geodesic, back into the dark, into space. He felt closed in, trapped. It was almost a claustrophobic feeling, a vague sense of uneasiness that brushed his heart, the pit of his stomach. He had never felt those things before, not even in the sweat lodge. All he knew was that he had to get out of there.

He found Sam and together they left the party, suited up. It wasn't until they left the geodesic that the pressure lifted from John. It had been all out of proportion to the situation.

He was still angry with himself because he hadn't stood up to the T.U.S.E. bureaucrat. The sense that he had betrayed something important weighed heavily upon him, yet on another level he felt there had been no choice. It was a bitter feeling. He was no better than the others.

He was a hypocrite.

\*

t was the first time John had been inside the computer bubble, the mobile command center for this operation. He wouldn't be there now if Sam hadn't talked him into it.

Sam was a friend of Carl Hegyer, who was running the board. The bubble hung well away from the station; they had a panoramic view. Sam had thought John might like to watch the spin from there. He admitted it was better than being with the brass in the center of the station, or watching it with the drunken revelers in the geodesic.

Spin was imparted to the station by an extremely simple and cheap method. The surface of the station was covered with thousands of small, one-shot aluminum trioxide rockets. The crew called them sparklers. They were dirty, but that didn't matter in space. What mattered was that they were cheap, composed of elements easily mined at the lunar complexes.

Through the programmed computer, Carl Hegyer could select the number and order of rocket firings. They would fire only a few at first, to get the station moving. Slowly they would increase the rotation by firing more and more rockets until the desired rate of spin was achieved. The point they were aiming for was that which would produce a fifty-g force at the rounded ends of the station. That would still leave the majority of rockets in reserve. The immediate area had been cleared in preparation for the firing. The geodesic party, still in full swing, had been unlocked from the station and moved a short distance away. Most of the

118

brass and dirtwalkers were in the swollen living quarters in the middle of the station.

The digital mounted next to the CRT screen on Carl's console ticked down. A signal flare soared across the darkness like an orange comet. The two-minute warning.

Carl broke the silence in the bubble. "All this will probably seem pretty anticlimactic," he said. "I'm not much more than the guy that pushes the plunger. It starts slow. Not much to see at first."

He was right. When the digital ran down to zero, Carl pointed to a few scattered dots on the station's image on the CRT screen. "Those are the rockets firing," he said. "We ought to be seeing something soon."

John looked out the large, curved port at the station. There were more rockets firing now, sending out white sparks like small magnesium flares. As he watched, one edge of the station occulted a star. It was moving. Still slow, but the movement was perceptible.

Although John had worked on several projects since his training, this was the first time he had seen his handiwork put into motion. It impressed him, moved him, touched something deep in his heart.

For this was wasicun, the work of the white man. Yet somehow, as the ponderous station gradually picked up speed with its trail of metallic sparks, it seemed more like the work of the People.

There was symmetry here, balance, purpose. There were circles, closed circles linked with the circular Earth. For a moment he forgot about the dirtwalkers on the station, the brawling party in the geodesic, the drunks and whores. Here was purpose, direction, in a fluid way. Relationships were being expressed that he could only guess at, not yet hold.

"It's beautiful," said Sam softly. "No one told me it would be beautiful."

John could only nod. He was afraid if he spoke, his voice would crack. Carl was busy at the console, fingers flying over the keyboard. Once in a while he would touch the CRT with a lightpen, triggering an individual rocket passed over.

It was going faster now, as fast as John had ever seen anything swing in space. He knew the station needed fifty-g's at the ends, zero-g at the center. It was necessary for the centrifugation and sedimentation of the material they were manufacturing. That seemed like a lot of g-forces, but the station was large, strong. It would handle it.

John saw it first, looking through the port. Carl saw it an instant later, through the computer. An unevenness, a ripple, spread through the pattern of the firing rockets. Suddenly the board went wild, every telltale in the room went from green to red. Outside the port, the universe was lit with a blinding white flash.

"Jesus Christ," cried Carl, frozen. "No!" A whole bank of rockets along one arm had fired at once. Not one rocket, not ten, but hundreds of them.

The station swung in a ballet of death, caught in an ungainly pirouette by the uneven forces. The wrenching stresses pulled at the station in a way that could have never been anticipated. The metal twisted, buckled, finally reached the breaking point and sheared. Before their horrified eyes, the station broke apart, one end of the barbell ripping away. It headed inexorably for the geodesic, a precise arc of destruction. The rest of the station, out of control, cartwheeled wildly away.

Time froze. John was held by fear, the old fear taught to him by Leonard Brokenfinger. It was the fear of one who can see with his heart, who can sense the spirits in the sweat lodge and in the vision pit. As bits of steel, aluminum, and boron silvered through space, catching the sun in their terrible dance, John became a *wichasha waken*. He saw through the eyes of his people, was one with everything around him, was in the center of the circle.

Those aboard the geodesic must have tried to get out of the way. Yet it happened too fast, they had no chance. John's people were in there, his spirit reached for them.

The terrible fear, the crawling fear broke through his heart. "Oh Wakan Tanka, Great

Mystery, all those people, don't let them die...." John felt the wings of Wakinyan Tanka, the great thunderbird. They were made out of the essence of darkness; they were as cold as ice, yet they burned his skin.

The geodesic was struck dead center. It burst apart as broken metal and broken people were ripped and scattered in a thousand different directions, tossing and tumbling end over end.

He heard himself screaming; it was as if he were back in the vision pit, and he remembered: *Wakinyan Tanka eats his young, for they make him many; yet he is still one. He has a huge beak filled with jagged teeth, yet he has no head. He has wings, yet he has no shape.*

From somewhere distant, Sam yelled: "Do something, Carl, do something."

From somewhere else, came Carl's voice: "I can't."

And Sam: "Save the others."

Carl: "I can't stop it. Calculations are too complex. I can't."

John felt the cold breaking of death, the death of all, Indian and wasicun alike. He broke, and was made whole. He pulled Carl from the chair, sat down in front of the computer console. Sam yelled, Carl screamed. These were disruptive forces; he blocked them out, ran his fingers lightly over the keyboard.

He touched a button and a single rocket

fired on the wildly careening remains of the station. He touched another button and a rocket fired someplace else on the skin of the station. There was a rhythm, a balance. Action and reaction, all parts of the whole.

Gently he felt his way into the heart of the computer. He did things, things happened. Forces were moved, stresses transposed from one place to another. It was all a matter of balance, of achieving a point of equilibrium. The computer was a prayer and he was in the pit again, close to the spirits that flickered in the dark and the thunder beings that carried the fear. His fingers danced over the keyboard. He felt, rather than saw, the forces he was manipulating. It was internal, not external—he was part and parcel of the things he did. He grabbed the lightpen and stroked the image of the runaway station on the screen. Under his fingers more rockets burst into life, counterbalancing the undesired motion. With the sureness of an ancient hand painting a Hopi jar, he sought out the proper forms, the pattern. The station slowed.

The fear, the ancient fear carried by prayer, was breaking him. It gave him the emptiness the wasicun built, transforming it into a wisdom. He frowned, added a few last strokes with the lightpen, tapped a few more buttons. The station stopped, motion arrested.

John slumped forward, drained of energy. He shook himself, looked around, half expecting to see the rolling desert, the towering mesas. Instead he saw Sam and Carl, though he didn't recognize them at first.

They stared at him with amazement, with fear, unable and unwilling to move, to break the spell. They could not comprehend what they had just seen.

John looked at them and understood that, and more. Much more. He stood.

"We'd better go," he said. "Some of them may still be alive."

They followed him. They would have followed him anywhere.

\*

It was cold on the mesa top; the sky was just beginning to lighten. The smoky dawn blurred the sharp pinpoints of stars and once again returned shape and substance to the world.

Leonard Broken-finger crouched on his haunches before the yawning opening of the vision pit. He held a leather bag that had belonged to his great-grandfather. But the bones and stones and roots and relics it contained were his own medicine. The medicine the spirits had given him in a dream.

The boy in the vision pit made stirring noises. His name was Jonas Goodbird, and he was barely more than a child. Now he was a man.

"You've been here four days," said

Broken-finger. "Your vision quest is over. I hope Wakan Tanka has helped you."

"I'm still alive," said Jonas in a quavering, unbelieving voice.

"Of course you are, though by all appearances, not by much." He made a gurgling sound deep in his throat, which was his way of laughing. As long as anyone in the tribe could remember, the medicine man had not smiled. Stories were told that his lips would break like pottery; and children still made a game of trying to get old Broken-finger to laugh and break his lips. They had never succeeded.

The boy was getting ready to leave the vision pit. It would take a few minutes for him to gather his wits. Broken-finger left him to this and walked to the edge of the mesa. He faced east. He was like a gnarled tree, already shaped by the wind.

The dry, cracked gullies stretched out below him, faded brown and red in the morning mist. He felt that this would be a good time to die. He was tired, yet strong. And it was not his time . . . not yet. He looked longingly at the towering rock formations below him. Those were the shapes of time. They did not have to bear the weight of flesh and spirit.

He thought of others he had walked down from the vision pit. There had been many. Some blurred into the darkness of deep memory, some stood out like figures carved out of light. He thought of John Stranger, gone now three winters, taken by the wasicun. He was special; the spirits clung to him like fire to good hard wood.

The sun broke the horizon.

He raised his arms to the heavens and stood that way for endless moments. He stared at the rising sun as if he were at sun dance.

He felt the cold brush of wings.

*Wakinyan Tanka. . . .*

*He has wings, yet has no shape.*

There were terrible things happening.

There were beautiful things happening.

It was a time of changes, a shifting of the order.

He felt the presence of the thunder beings and a profound, empty sadness. Arms still high, tears ran down his cheeks.

Yet he smiled for the first time in fifty years. The mere presence of the ancient spirit creatures was a sign.

He would live a little longer. His people would survive a little longer.

His lips cracked and blood ran down his chin, dribbling onto his brown yet frail chest.

And he thought of John Stranger.

*

They arrived at the ruined station before the summoned rescue vehicles. From the outside it looked to be the disaster it was. The end that had torn off left jagged remains, a twisted mass of beams, wires, and pipes. John led them to the living quarters in what had once been the middle of the station. It appeared intact but had been under considerable stress. What g-forces it had been subjected to could only be guessed at.

It was pitch-black inside; the air was stale but breathable. John flipped back his visor and turned on his lantern. He could hear low moans. Moans meant life.

And what of life, of death? His people had died in the geodesic; he had been unable to help them. Those that lived, those he saved, were of the wasicun. He had done what had to be done, led by the thunder spirits. There were reasons for everything.

His lamp stabbed through the blackness. Bodies floated in horrible, contorted shapes. Here and there an arm waved, a leg moved. Twisted wreckage was everywhere.

They worked together quietly, with purpose. They separated the living from the dead, did whatever they could for those who hung in between. Some they lost, some they saved. John drifted to the floor grid. It was twisted and buckled—people were trapped there. He worked at freeing them.

A soft voice called his name. A hand touched his shoulder. Anna. She lived.

"I thought you were dead," he said. "Dead with the others on the geodesic."

"I . . . I came here. It was . . ." Her voice trailed off.

Suddenly the chamber was filled with light as the rescue crew entered. They were efficient and noisy, barking orders everywhere. They took over. A part of John relaxed. In the bright light, Anna looked terrible. The side of her face was purple with a large bruise, her left arm hung at a funny angle. She was staring intently at him.

"You've changed," she said, slowly reaching out with her other hand to stroke the side of his face. There was awe in her voice, tinged with fear. She saw in his face things of the People. It was like looking into the past through the eyes of her mother's mother. There were things there that frightened her, things that made her proud.

"I am what I always have been," John said.

He saw many things, good and bad. The wasicun controlled his body, but not his spirit. There were things to be done and he had been called to do them. It would be a difficult time, but a good time for the People.

The cold wings of Wakinyan Tanka brushed his soul. The thunderbird would be with him always, as it was in the instant of death, the instant of salvation. He was part of the circle, perhaps in the center.

A long road lay ahead. He had but taken
the first step.

---

```
5641   //STRANGER JOB
5642   (3014,5002,1,1,0), 'COL=1, CAP#3', CLASS=Q
5643   //EXEC WATFIV
5644
5645   $JOB
5646   STRANGER, JOHN SOC 187735-NN-000
5647   TRANS-UNITED BILLET OZMA
5648
5649   ACCESS CLASSIFICATION LEVEL THREE CONFIDENTIAL
5650   PASSWORD: REDMAN
5651
5652   STOCHASTIC ANALYSIS FOLLOWS
5653
5654   INTUITIVE RIGHT CHOICES IN DOUBLE BLIND SITUATIONS
5655   TRIALS = 100
5656   SUCCESS RATE = 100%
5657
5658   KINESTHESIC AWARENESS
5659   TRIALS = 100
5660   SUCCESS RATE = 100%
5661
5662   PROBABILITY THIS DUE TO CHANCE APPROACHES ZERO
5663
5664   CONCLUSION:
5665   SUBJECT INTUITIVELY MAKES CORRECT DECISIONS IN
5666      APPARENTLY AMBIGUOUS SITUATIONS.
5667   SUBJECT HAS HIGH AWARENESS OF SURROUNDINGS AND
5668      RELATIONSHIPS BETWEEN OBJECTS IN HIS ENVIRONMENT.
5669
```

```
5670   NOTE: SUBJECT UNCOOPERATIVE
5671
5672   WEAKNESS: TRIBAL LOYALTY
5673   CLOSE RELATIONS:
5674   LEONARD BROKEN-FINGER SOC 15782-NN-863
5675   ANNA GRASS-LIKE-LIGHT SOC 16364-NN-347
5676   SAM WOQUINI SOC 13827-NN-676
5677   EXPLOIT WITH EXTREME CARE
5678
5679   THIS SUBJECT IS POTENTIALLY DANGEROUS
5680   THIS SUBJECT IS POTENTIALLY USEFUL
5681
5682   RECOMMENDATION: OBSERVATION, MANIPULATION & CONTROL
5683
5684   /*ROUTE PRINT REMOTE 7
5685   STOP
5686   END
5687   2 NOV 2180—9:14 AM
5688/*
END    SOC 187735FILE-NN-000
```

Director Gerard Lincoln Smith Leighton
sat in the vast darkness of his office in the
Bernal sphere space colony that was his
fiefdom.

Here, upon what was ostensibly Trans-
United property, he had built a grandiose
villa to symbolize his power and status; if
he could be compared to a modern-day Lo-
renzo de' Medici, then this villa was his *Poggio a Caiano*, that architectual dream of the

Renaissance humanists. Leighton's own Ivy House was built to impress heads of states, directors, CEO's, and other princes, to facilitate the constant and delicate diplomacy between governments and states and duchies and corporations and other powerful and dangerous legal entities. Leighton's villa was in fact modeled on *Poggio a Caiano*, but on a much larger scale. It was also built to be a temporary escape from the crushing responsibilities of the directorship of the world's most powerful corporation.

Leighton had inherited a nation-state which had no borders. He was a corporate prince, a slave to the unceasing demands of client states and individuals demanding or begging for any one of a myriad benefices and offices and sponsorships with which the corporation rewarded its faithful. That was how the system worked ... on patronage and short-term alliances.

But for this moment, Leighton had escaped. It was as if he were floating in his cushioned chair, for he had keyed walls, floor, and ceiling to transparency and was staring into the hard, ice-clear beauties of near-Earth space.

He had turned the room into an eyepiece of the Trans-United orbiting telescope.

The constellations blazed around him, as if the universe was indeed the inside of a great sphere—or as the ancients had proposed, a dark firmament punctured with millions of tiny holes through which passed those few rays of the celestial light. Around him were his factories that grew crystals and purified metals; refined here were foam steel and iron-lead alloys, which had the most interesting electrical properties. It was in these laboratories and factories that liquid-state physics had become a reality. Leighton nodded, as if affirming that all this was real, for it had been his dream.

But what gave him the most pleasure was the university that rotated in the sector beyond the labs and factories. He had devoted himself to it, and was repaid, for Leighton-Loyola University had eclipsed Oxford-Harvard as the most prestigious center of learning and scholarship. It was a world all to itself, a mirrored Stanford torus rotating in the primordial darkness, where thousands of scientists and engineers lived and did the research that would begin a new Renaissance. Or so Leighton dreamed.

Beside it was the Cup-and-Saucer, the radio telescope that had received the enigmatic radio signal from the triple-sun system 36 Ophiuchi, which had come to be known as the Rosetta Triptych. Part of that transmission was apparently a blueprint for a faster-than-light drive, but there were still too many missing pieces of information.

And then there were the recent incidents

of mass hallucinations and hysteria on Earth.

Leighton wondered, as did many others, if one were related to the other.

He keyed down the magnification and looked into another quadrant. A crew was doing routine maintenance on a satellite.

He focused in on its crew master, John Stranger, and contemplated what he would do with him.

Stranger was a useful tool, but a difficult one to manipulate.

He was hard to break.

But he *would* be broken.

\*

Leonard Broken-finger had not eaten in four days.

Sitting cross-legged on his coarsely woven star blanket, his back resting against a hard wall of red pipestone rock that towered over him, the old man felt as light and empty as a gourd. He had a small skin of water beside him, but he used it sparingly; he had passed the stages of feeling thirst or hunger.

Broken-finger had come to this place deep in the deadlands of the North Dakota reservation to speak with the spirit of his father. The old man was troubled and needed wisdom.

This was a good place, for it was in the very bowels of *Uncegila*, the fabled monster whose ancient bones had been turned into the cliffs and canyons and stone seracs of this lifeless place. Spirits were thick in the air here, like the clouds of sandflies at dusk, for many years ago the ghost dancers had come here to roll up the world with their prayers. But it had not yet been the time for miracles, and the ghost dancers died, their bones becoming part of *Uncegila*'s own.

Broken-finger had made many vision quests in his lifetime, had even been buried once for seven days when he visited the dead. But this visit to the spirit world would probably be his last. He smiled, thanking the Great Mystery, for he was once again like a young man seeking a vision.

As the sun moved through the sky, the shadows in the deep canyons shifted, creating a new world in chiaroscuro. Broken-finger stared unblinkingly as the line of darkness crept like sleep toward the wide ledge where he sat. Far away a rock cracked as it cooled in the shadows.

But the sun would not set for hours.

He listened to the wind wheezing through twisted canyons, and wondered if it was a spirit or happenstance. He felt the sunlight baking his face and chest and remembered looking into the sun for a vision every year at sun dance. But the youth who had danced and pulled at the leather thong piercing his chest lived only in memory now. He remembered the words he used to sing:

*I am standing*
*In a sacred way*
*Fire is my face*
*The Earth is my center*

An ant crawled upon Broken-finger's shoulder. He was aware of the ant, but he felt as if he, too—like the spirits of the ghost dancers—had become *Uncegila*. Had become like stone itself.

The ant crossed his forehead and disappeared into his white hair, held in place by a faded red bandanna.

He waited for the spirit of his father.

He sang.

Before him, Broken-finger had carefully placed a few offerings on the ancient star blanket. A piece of raw liver had dried to crust in a small earthenware bowl; that was for the spirit of his father, in case he was hungry. Beside the bowl were a few grains of corn and a flint-tipped arrow; its brightly colored, cloth stringers hung lifelessly from its shaft. Broken-finger wore his leather pouch of holy medicine on a strap around his neck. He had drawn sacred symbols in the sand to the four directions so the spirits would know he was within the circle.

Although he was old and dried-out and had liked women too much when he was younger and stronger, he was still a *wichasha waken*, a medicine man. He only hoped that the spirits would remember.

As the shadow of the lip of the canyon touched the western edge of his blanket, a lizard the color of pipestone appeared out of the shadow of a nearby rock and stopped before him. The holy man did not blink; nor did he turn his head, not even when the tiny reptile began to grow and change.

It expanded, as if it were solid smoke.

It displaced all warmth and life.

It soon towered above him.

Its keratinous scales formed great spines, which fused and swelled into naphthol black wings the size of mizzen sails.

Wings that beat the air so hard that Broken-finger could only think of bellows. . . .

And the thunder beings.

The old man held a single eagle feather in his right hand, a carved piece of wood in his left, and prayed.

The thunder being stared deep into Broken-finger's eyes.

Another rock cracked in the distance.

The old man could feel the presence of his father, who spoke through the thunder being. Broken-finger stared into the eyes of the monster who carried his father's spirit, for if he turned away or became afraid, he would certainly die.

The canyon was quiet, yet the old Lakota words hung in the air like dust.

"I am troubled, father," Broken-finger said, staring at the thunder being, which was now transforming itself into its true aspect: ebon nothingness, a vast and vertiginous emptiness. "I am afraid for John Stranger, and for his friends."

A few seconds passed, or maybe an hour.

"Yes, my father," said Broken-finger, now wrapped in darkness even as he sweltered in the heat of the afternoon sun. "I know that. Anna Grass-like-light believes she has left the circle, but the circle is larger than she can imagine. Sam Woquini is wild, *ikce wicasa*, but he is our own. He has not forgotten how to dream without sleep, and he still carries a pipe. But John Stranger has doubts, and he is in the center of the circle. His life carries the life of our people. If only wasicun had not taken him so soon ... I could have taught him to use his medicine. But he has learned much in the heavens."

There was a movement, and Broken-finger could see, as if he were looking through the wrong end of a telescope, that the lizard had moved. It seemed to be a tiny focus of life in the center of the empty vortex of smoky darkness that was the thunder being.

"Yes, father," the old man said, nodding, "I still have the dreams. I still see the frozen faces of our people, those who are not dead and not alive. But I also see something new, something that is like the spirits, yet is not. In some of my dreams I see the spirits of my ancestors and the *wazyia*, which is terrible enough; but some of these dreams are so bright that I feel blinded when I awaken. I am afraid of these dreams . . . they feel *wowakan*. Unnatural. I have given much thought to them, but their meanings have not yet been revealed to me."

A moment passed. A shadow moved across the blanket. Broken-finger felt a cold breeze flowing around him. "I see," he said. "Yes, I remember the stories you used to tell me. I will do as you ask. I am not afraid to seek Corn Woman and the Sandman." He smiled. "I can still use colored sand as medicine. But am I not too old to fight ice with fire? It is not for me that I fear the cold . . . I fear death for our people."

A deer looked down from the canyon rim, then turned and disappeared, as if frightened.

"*Washtay*," Broken-finger said, which was the old Lakota word for good. "Then I will do that. I will ask Jonas Goodbird to help me. And I will wait for those whom you will send. I will do it the old way, just as you showed me when I was a child. Yes, father, I remember the words. They are still clear in my mind."

Then the thunder being swallowed itself, like smoke being sucked into a great vortex, leaving in its place only heat and rock and sunlight and the pipestone-colored lizard.

The smell of death settled around the

medicine man like a cold, hard fist. He could feel—almost taste—the sharp metallic tang of the spiritless weapons of death the wasicun spun like complex mechanical tops in great circles in the sky, far above where the eagles soared. He could see John Stranger, fighting for his life and the lives of his people. A part of John's life was ending, and another was starting. There were many roads it could take. Most ended with his death.

Broken-finger slowly reached out and touched the lizard with the eagle feather. "Goodbye, my father." He took the rest of the corn and chanted as he threw the seeds to the four directions.

> These four are my relatives
> We are all related
> We are all one

He ro led the rest of his things inside the blanket and took a small sip of water. Then he got to his feet. His muscles were cramped, and his knees cracked.

Broken-finger took one last look around and felt at peace. The lizard had disappeared. But it had been good talking to his father's spirit. When he had walked the Earth, he had been a strange and distant man.

He had not changed much since he died.

\*

139

6347   ACCESS CLASSIFICATION LEVEL THREE CONFIDENTIAL
6348
6349
6350   UPDATE FILE: JOHN STRANGER
6351
6352   SOC 187735-NN-000
6353   TRIBE LOCATION: D5-SOUTH DAKOTA-116
6354   DRAFT DATE: 7 APR 2177
6355   STATUS: PERMANENT DRAFTEE (INVOLUNTARY)
6356   TIME REMAINING ON CONTRACT: INDEFINITE
6357   WORK LEVEL: BELLMAN, NEAR-EARTH ORBITAL CONSTRUCTION
6358
6359   STAN;
6360   THIS IS JUST FOR YOUR INFORMATION, BUT LEIGHTON
6361   HAS TAGGED THIS GUY FOR OBSERVATION. HE'S HEADING A
6362   TEAM OF FLOATERS THAT WILL BE IN YOUR QUAD AND I
6363   THOUGHT YOU OUGHT TO KNOW THEY'RE GOING TO BE
6364   WATCHING HIM CLOSELY. THAT MEANS THEY'RE GOING TO
6365   BE WATCHING YOU, TOO. DON'T FUCK THIS ONE UP. I'M
6366   NOT SURE WHY THE OLD MAN HAS TAKEN SUCH AN INTEREST
6367   IN HIM, BUT THEY'VE GOT HIM NAILED BUT GOOD. SOME
6368   SORT OF TROUBLEMAKER, I GUESS. ALL HIS RECORDS
6369   ARE FLAGGED, SO BURN THIS FLIMSY AFTER YOU READ IT.
6370   HOPE TO SEE YOU THE NEXT TIME I GET OUT THAT WAY.
6371   THINGS ARE ABOUT THE SAME HERE, BUSY AS USUAL. SAME
6372   OLD STUFF. TAKE CARE, AND WATCH YOUR ASS ON THIS
6373   ONE.
6374                                                          FRANK
6375
6376
6377   /*ROUTE PRINT REMOTE 65
6378   STOP
6379   END
6380

6381   3 JAN 2181   7:34 AM
6382   SOC 187735 NOFILE WIPE/DISK *** FLIMSY ONLY ***
/END


FILE NOTE:

  THE ABOVE INTERCEPTED ON NET 53, 3 JAN 2181, 7:34:15 AM.

ACTION:

  FRANK DREXLER TERMINATED WITH PREJUDICE
  STAN HAWKINS TRANSFERRED ASTEROID MINING COMPLEX 53-YT

---

John Stranger drifted in the blazing star-filled night as he watched his crew crawl over the surface of the satellite like a handful of ants on a silver, spiny barbell. They were almost finished, and it looked like they'd be about forty hours ahead of schedule. This one had been simple: replace a few solar cells and attend to a module that had deteriorated because of an acid leak. He wished they could all be so easy, but it never worked out that way. Each gravy run was invariably followed by a ball buster. It would probably be a furnace or the remoras next. Soon his easygoing crew would be raw with tension, including Sam Woquini, who bragged that any duty was just *sleep-time* for him.

"Hey, Bellman," called a voice through the static. It was Mike Elliot, John's immediate superior.

"Yeah, you got him," John said.

"Shift channel," ordered Elliot, using his rank to grind John whenever the occasion presented itself.

Damn, John thought, tonguing to confidential. It had to be trouble.

"I've got some new orders for you, Stranger," Elliot said. "You're on your way to sector omega-ten."

"No fucking way," John said. "After what my crew went through last month, they have a right to some safe duty. And I know goddamn well that omega-ten's all watchdogs, most of them sentries. Cluster bombs, for Christ's sake. I'm not completely crazy. Send some other unit."

"You're available and it's you they're sending," Elliot said. He always sounded condescending when he was enjoying himself. "The orders have already been cut."

"Put me on report if you want, I'm not doing it. I'll be fucked if I'm taking my people in there without a weapons team."

"The papers were signed by Director Leighton himself," Elliot said in a sickeningly smooth voice. He knew he had John by the balls; Leighton was the one man you couldn't buck. John could imagine Elliot's baby face, looking serious, as if he wasn't really getting a charge out of this.

"When does this duty start?"

"Right now. Gather up your crew. We've assigned you some extra people. And you'll need a briefing with Murphy."

"If they're not weapons people, I don't want them. New people just get in the way."

"You work with who I tell you to work with, Stranger." Elliot broke the connection with a loud snap.

John opened a channel to Sam Woquini. "Did you get that?"

"I couldn't resist tapping in," Sam said. "I already got Anna, so don't worry. Look, we've slept our way through all the other missions, and we're still here to tell the tale, so don't worry about it. I'm getting the sled now. Be there in a few minutes."

John watched his friend, who was a distant white speck blinking in and out of the darkness, move toward the sled. Everything out here was either deep black or blinding white, except the distant stars, which shone steadily. Some of the pinpoints of light appeared ruddy, others were blue white or copper. The heavens were like massive fireworks caught in stop-motion.

All around John small satellites with huge fans of solar cells hung in orbit. In the distance were the L-3 and L-5 habitats surrounded by factories and labs, and the ever-present debris that seemed to gather around them.

John bit his lip as he watched Sam pick up the rest of the crew. His people weren't rested enough to work the watchdogs, not yet. They needed more time. Omega-ten was a crowded and complicated sector, a real bitch.

Too many things could go wrong.

\*

Ray Murphy was feeding numbers into the computer as John watched the greenish hologram flicker into life. It was a three-dimensional representation of the omega-ten sector, with color-coded points of light identifying the various objects in orbit within the area. It was too crowded, there were too many points of light, too much debris. Red bands crisscrossed the sphere, indicating microwave transmission pathways to be avoided at all costs. There were too many red bands. There was too much of everything except empty space.

"This is what omega-ten will look like when you enter," Ray said. "We're clearing vector seven five for your approach pattern." He tapped in a few more numbers and a yellow beam appeared, running diagonally through the hologram.

"Give me real time," John asked without looking up.

Ray made some adjustments, and the points of light began to move. It was a complicated picture, orbits swinging in every direction. A watchdog's orbit constantly changed to lessen the chance of someone destroying it. Debris and space-junk drifted through the sector, each piece watched as closely as the satellites, for in the wrong place they could be just as deadly. To the uninitiated, the hologram was mass confusion; to John Stranger it was a delicately balanced system, a ballet of vectors in space; a balance felt rather than seen, in a way he could not describe.

But something was wrong, a pinpoint of light moving against the flow.

"There it is," John said. "That's the one."

Ray nodded. "Watchdog 26-BCC. Sentry-class watchdog. Cluster bomb. We're having trouble keeping control. In fact, we may be losing it entirely. There's a good chance it's already snatched."

John felt wired, nervous. He didn't like this at all. A sentry-class watchdog with cluster bombs was the worst of a bad lot. A snatched one was a nightmare. There was absolutely no telling what it might do.

The original watchdogs had been sent up as spy satellites to monitor ground activities and serve as early warning systems. The move to armed, sentry-class *peacekeeping* machines was swift and quiet in the years following the two-hour period in which ninety percent of Iraq was pounded into rubble in retaliation for a chemical warfare attack that killed every living thing within twenty miles of Tel Aviv.

Ironically, the rain of death came from what had been thought to be a weather satellite. It had been constructed and launched for Israel by Macro Technologies.

When countries went into space to protect their borders they turned to the corporations that had experience in space. Organizations such as GTE, Macro, ComSat, and Trans-United had been building satellites for years. The corporations already had the hardware, the research teams, and their own launch vehicles. This arrangement allowed them to become as wealthy and powerful as nation-states.

But before the nation-states could react, the delicate balance of world power had shifted. Shifted completely, irretrievably.

A new age had dawned.

Nations could no longer be certain who controlled their satellites. Even the smallest corporations had the ability to wipe out entire countries or the ground bases of competitors.

Now corporations and nation-states alike participated in a covert but deadly war. . . .

Snatching was the gaining of control of someone else's satellite. It involved deci-

146

phering the codes that controlled the satellite and overriding the original programs with your own.

Sentry-class watchdogs, because of the weapons they carried, were prime candidates for a snatch. Even though satellite technology was extremely sophisticated, watchdogs were snatched more often than anyone was willing to admit. It was often an inside job. People such as Ray were watched closely to protect them from being kidnapped and to keep them from selling out. Trust was a rare commodity among those who dealt with the doomsday machines.

"We may have lost it last week," Ray said. "I just don't know. It follows some commands, but not others. It may be a malfunction, or it may be something else."

"Yes," John said, feeling cold and nervous. "It may be something else, all right. Give me a look inside the watchdog."

As he looked into the holo, at the images of circuitry and machinery, he felt that he was already in the omega-ten sector, carefully dancing with death.

*

Leonard Broken-finger stood on the edge of a deep ravine in the center of the reservation. The ground was striated umber and rust; it was dry and lifeless, as dry as the still air that seemed to suck the very moisture out of him. His face was wrinkled and the color of pipestone; his body looked as desiccated as the land. But he was as strong as the distant rock towers that the ancients had thought were the whitened bones of a great, primeval monster. He was implacable as the stones underfoot.

He watched two young boys stalking a rabbit in the dusty, dry rush below him. They carried sticks with charred, pointed ends. Broken-finger knew them well, and he felt a profound sadness well up inside him. Soon, they would be taken away by the corporations, drafted into service to work behind desks or in space. The corporation could extend a draftee's tour for nearly any reason at all. All because of a long-ago conscription treaty made with the government, a contract that could be bent, broken, and twisted in a thousand ways. But the corporation had all the power: they owned the land.

When the boys returned—if they ever returned at all—they would behave like strangers.

So very few had had the old talents, the medicine spirit, and they were all but gone now. Gray Fox and Afraid-of-Bears had died working in space for wasicun. Their bodies were never even returned for proper burial. Broken-finger imagined that their souls floated in the sky like ghostly stars. They could have brought strength and resolution to their people, but they never had the chance.

Russell Inkanish had felt the spirit early; he was barely eight years old. Broken-finger had devoted himself to him, but it wasn't enough. The corporation drafted him when he was eighteen; he came back four years later, a narcodrine junkie who wandered the desert like the other spirits that could sometimes be seen flickering and ghosting through the deadlands on moonlit nights.

John Stranger had been the strongest. He had seen the spirits as light in the vision pit. He had screamed in the sweat lodge when the heat blistered his back. He could have been a *wichasha waken*, a medicine man. But he, too, had been taken too soon. There were times when Broken-finger could still feel John's presence. He had been gone a long time. Broken-finger had the strong intuition that the corporation was using John for a different purpose than any of the others; they were testing him, as he himself had done many times in the past. John had never failed Broken-finger. He had many things in front of him . . . if he could survive.

Broken-finger stood as still as stone. He stared at the sun, but didn't burn with the terrible heat that poured down upon him. Tired of chasing the rabbit, the boys had returned to the village. Broken-finger noticed nothing, yet missed nothing.

He was thinking of John Stranger.

John was in the center of the circle, which was broken. Broken-finger could see the circle in the blinding whiteness of the sun. Images played in the white fire. He saw fire falling from the sky, killing hundreds; and John's hand was on the fire bolts. How could that be?

And Broken-finger felt the coldness of living corpses beneath him, as if the very stuff he was standing on were made of human bone and sinew. It was as if the dead were below him; yet they were not dead. They were now spirit.

He felt a vague brushing and thought of Anna Grass-like-light. Something dangerous and strong and sad was working inside her. She was with John. There were others, too. He could feel their presence as pain. He could see them burning, as he stared into the sun.

Many would soon die.

Broken-finger shivered and blinked. Now the sun was far to the west. He tried to move, and felt the familiar brush of cold wings. The vision that was given to him at his first vision quest many years ago returned once more. He shook with the vision, seeing it once again, for it was as real as the ground upon which he stood. He cried in joy and terror as he faced its beauty and power. He saw the creature of myth and dreams, the greatest of thunder beings, the being that can be seen but not comprehended. He saw his own dream of it, a dream that changed with his every thought and prayer.

*Wakinyan Tanka eats his own young, for they make him many; yet he is one. He has a huge beak filled with jagged teeth, yet he has no head. He has wings, yet has no shape.*

Broken-finger prayed for John and the others.

He blinked again and it was dark. The day was gone, as if absorbed into John's burning eyes. The sky was filled with stars. Perhaps John and his people were one of those floating points of light. Broken-finger gazed east, toward the village. He wanted the company and comfort of his family, but instead he walked toward the flashing neon of the corporation-owned commissary.

\*

John Stranger sat by himself in a videotect booth in the orbiting pleasure-dome, but he was not hooked in. He didn't need to lose himself in the videos, which were simulated experiences, mostly sexual. He just wanted to be alone. He left the booth on transparency, but turned off the outside noise. All he could hear was faint thunder.

151

Broken-finger used to say it was the thunder beings whispering to him. It was more likely the result of an old ear infection he had had when he was a child.

He looked out through the transparency at the rows of iron bandits and telefac booths on the casino floor. There were also telefac games, where winners received a jolt of electric pleasure and losers had their nights spoiled with bone-crushing migraines; and there were traditional gaming tables, such as roulette, chuck-a-luck, craps, hazard, liar dice, vingt-et-un, and slide.

On this floor the crowd was mostly floaters, although corporate executives and their consorts drifted through, slumming. The more expensive and more deadly pleasures were upstairs, where the organ gambling and deformation games were being played. But they were closed to floaters. What the first level provided, though, was house whores—natural men and women; birdmen with implanted genitalia and feathers the color of rainbows; geishas; androgynes; drag queens and kings; children; machines promising clean, cold sex, although their exposed organs were fleshy; and all manner of genetically engineered mooncalves.

It was obvious that the providers didn't believe that a floater could think about anything above the groin. Perhaps they were right, John thought. He saw Shorthair take a drink from a robot that had the logo of the Trans-United Corporation emblazoned on its chest. Inside the sweep of the *T* and the *U* someone had painted a poorly executed fist with an extended middle finger. Shorthair had his arm around a naked woman whose skin was bleached zinc white. Thick artificial strands of glossy black hair curled around her head, moving like snakes, as if they had a life of their own. She looked pubescent.

John watched them disappear into the crowd. A fight started in the area of the iron bandits, and the M.P.'s took their time before breaking it up.

The reservation seemed an eternity away. It was no wonder that so many of John's people became, in effect, white men. It was easy to do; they were far from anything that could be called home. They were white man's tools, living in a white man's universe. John could not blame those who became lost in the frogskin world. In fact, he felt as lost as they did.

Anna Grass-like-light found John's booth and stood in front of it, staring in. Her eyes looked glazed and unfocused and she was trembling. John had the sudden and disquieting thought that insects were moving beneath her skin, causing her subtle, yet grotesque facial expressions. She had done too many narcodrines. Anna pounded on the transparent walls, and John came out of the booth and took her to a table where they sat across from each other. She ordered a drink from a mobile vendor, then spilled part of it when she set her glass down onto the table.

"Having fun in there?" she asked, fumbling in her pocket for a narcodrine, a large bluish capsule. John stopped her before she could twist and break it under her nose.

"Leave it alone for a while," John said. "You're fucked-up enough already. You look like a walking overdose."

"Fuck you, medicine man. We're about to get our asses blown up in a sentry and you're worried about some poppers? Maybe you don't need anything to cut through the shakes. You're so caught up in the old ways, you think you can just have a dream and we'll all be safe."

She popped the narcodrine. For an instant Anna seemed to soften, and John remembered her as she used to be planetside. He'd known her since they were children. She had a sweetness about her that had all but disappeared after she was drafted.

"What the hell are you doing here, anyway?" she asked. "You told me you had to be alone to get ready for tomorrow. You lied to me."

"I just couldn't stay in the barrack any longer," John said defensively. She had caught him. If they were going to survive tomorrow, he would have to put his thoughts right, dream about it, work out every detail. But he couldn't seem to concentrate in his room, even though it was quiet. Perhaps it was too quiet, because he hadn't been able to visualize his mnemonic of the watchdog. In a way, Anna had been right about John having a dream and making everyone safe. He certainly owed it to them to try.

"Why not?" Anna asked.

"I don't know," John said.

"So you came here to slum it up."

"I thought it would help to be nearby," John said lamely, "in case there's any trouble."

"You're a fucking liar," Anna said. A tic was working like a bug that had been lodged in a vein in her neck. "You came here for the same reason the rest of us did. You're scared out of your suit. So you thought that if you could see the rest of us behaving like assholes, you'd feel better. That would get your thoughts back into line real quick, wouldn't it?"

John couldn't answer. She knew him well and had touched a nerve. He couldn't stand to think of himself as a prig, but there it was.

"Do you want to fuck me, medicine man?" Anna asked softly, an edge of desperation and pleading in her voice, although her face seemed hard and angry as she looked at him.

It was an old challenge. Anna had played it before. But John had made a vow. He wasn't going to live his life on white man's terms, even if it meant staying celibate. He had to keep to the red path. He had to be the measure for the others.

"You're such a fucking hypocrite," Anna said. "I'll admit to being scared and lonely. But you, you've got a dead heart."

"Come on, I'll get you home."

"The fuck if you will," Anna said, and she stood up, looked around, then called over a whore whose skin was covered with fur like a bear. She leaned against him as he helped her away from John.

John wanted to go after her, but he couldn't, for the mnemonic of the watchdog began to spin in his mind like a perfectly transparent geode. Everything around him became peripheral, and his sight, which was now clear and focused, turned inward.

In that instant, John Stranger hated himself for what he had become . . . for what they had all become.

\*

The trail was not difficult to follow, even at night. Although the moon had not yet risen, the air was clear and the panoply of stars provided all the light Broken-finger needed. He took comfort in the distant howling of wild dogs and the night sounds

of owls and insects and scurrying creatures. He paused for several minutes and
stared at the fluted towers and rills of a
small canyon, all seen as shadows of different intensity. The darkest shadows in the
twisted canyon were hard and cold, and he
knew them well. Once he had come here to
seek answers from his ancestors. He had
stayed over a week without food or water,
and although forty years had passed since
then, he knew he could walk the canyon
blindfolded and never miss a step. Time had
become compressed for Broken-finger. He
could remember what he had done years
ago with the same clarity that he remembered yesterday's events.

As he crested the last ridge, he saw the
commissary and started downhill. It blazed
like some sort of aberration of the northern
lights. The commissary was built of logs, in
keeping with some of the old ways. It sat in
an island of concrete surrounded by parked
steam cars and the small scoots favored by
the young braves. Music drifted across the
parking lot.

When Broken-finger walked through the
door, he found the sounds of music and
laughter and shouting deafening after the
whispers of wind through stone in the desert night.

The large room was packed with young
people from the reservation and visitors.
Most were dancing or sitting at tables. Too

many were drunk or stoned. Along the far wall was a row of videotect caskets, which were all in use. Broken-finger could see shadowy figures moving to preprogrammed hallucinations inside each casket; and it made him shudder to think they were bloods he had known since infancy. Incongruously placed between the row of caskets was a stone fireplace. The stones were real, but the fireplace was not. A holo of flames flickered in the hearth, and the sounds of wood crackling had almost fooled Broken-finger the first time he was in the commissary. The other walls were covered with softly lit, enticing pictures of food items and general supplies. He could smell the items and hear the olfactories sigh as he passed each picture. If one wanted flour or boots or jewelry, one only had to press the picture, insert an ID credit card, and the stuff would be delivered, wrapped tightly in plastic, from some mysterious basement. Broken-finger had never used the machines, but he had watched many old men and women of his tribe stand in front of the wall as if they were at market. It's just another way to make us weak, he thought. Instead of growing corn, we push pictures. The machines were, in fact, about twenty years obsolete. But Broken-finger didn't know or care. He would rather walk twelve miles and buy from the one-armed man who had a blind wife—he knew many good stories.

A white man standing behind a long wooden counter looked up as Broken-finger approached him. He looked middle-aged and paunchy. Most of the whites working on the reservation were doing punishment duty. "What can I do for you, chief?" he asked, wiping the counter with his hand, obviously a compulsive habit.

"I'm not a chief," he said evenly. "I wish to place a call to John Stranger. He is a bell-man for Trans-United. My name is Leonard Broken-finger. My last name is two words separated by a dash. You'll need to know that when you write it in your machine."

"ID card."

Broken-finger handed him a gray card.

"I take it he's topside, now," said the man.

"John Stranger is wherever Trans-United has sent him."

"Thanks for all your help," the man said sarcastically. He typed onto a keyboard behind the counter. "The satellite link is pretty good tonight, but it may take awhile."

Broken-finger just nodded and waited. A group of young people waved him over to their table. Then they made faces at him, told him stupid jokes, and finally Stan Walking, who was a good boy, begged him to crack a smile. "Come on," Stan said. "Let me at least win the bet. You've got to put on a happy face sometime."

159

"What is it you hear from your sister?" he asked Stan.

"She's all right, I guess. Trans-United transferred her again. Somewhere in South America. In Paraguay. Asunción, or somewhere like that."

"That's the third time this year," Broken-finger said.

"She doesn't care," Stan said. "One office is the same as the other, I guess. She signed up for another five-year hitch. Said the money's pretty good."

Broken-finger nodded.

"Your call is ready," said the man behind the counter. "Take it in the back booth."

Broken-finger walked around the counter and stepped into the plastic booth, which immediately darkened. The door slid shut with a creaking noise behind him. Then slowly the image of John Stranger resolved about four feet away from him. Broken-finger had no sense of the cubicle he was in; it was as if he and John were in a large room.

"Broken-finger," John said. "It's been—"

"I bring you news of your father. He is not well." John's father had been dead for almost twenty years.

"Wait a minute," John said, and he leaned forward. For an instant, he was out of view. Then there was a buzzing noise; and when John's image returned, it seemed to shimmer. "There," he said. "I've attached a scrambler. If anybody's listening in, they'll get only static."

Broken-finger didn't seem to notice. "Your father has a high fever, and his mind is not well. He has many dreams and speaks them to me. They make no sense, but I promised him I would tell them to you."

"My father?" John asked.

"He fears the fire from the sky," Broken-finger said. "It brings death to his descendants and his people, and somehow your hand is on the fire. He sees that this is not your doing, but that you have been forced into this thing. He trusts your judgment, though. It is a silly dream, of course, but I have promised him."

"I don't understand," John said.

"He sees more. He is worried for you and Grass-like-light and Sam Woquini. Red Feather is cold on his heart. There is danger for your people. He sees a village of frozen faces."

"We're all going out tomorrow," John said. "A watchdog has somehow—"

"Your father knows nothing of watchdogs. He knows only the things I have told you. You will have to make a decision and it will be painful. Death will be all around you like steam in the sweat lodge. You must make your decision and not look back. You must not punish yourself for the thing you have done. This is what your father told to me in the heat of his fever. They are ramblings of an old man. But I have given my word to tell these things to you."

"And you, Broken-finger. Are you okay?"

"I am simply an old man who carries a message from another to you. Your father sees one more thing in his fever. He sees you leading your people."

"I do that every day. It's my job as bell-man."

"Yes, John Stranger, that is your job. I must go now. Your father is not well."

"My father—"

"Take care, John Stranger," and then Broken-finger pressed the disconnect button that glowed on a faint console beside him. The image of John Stranger disappeared as the lights in the booth came on and the door creaked open.

\*

Director Leighton's office occupied the entire top shell of O'Neil Seven. The expansive curved ceiling was over ten meters high, a conspicuous waste of space that served to intimidate those who had to do business with him in person. The ceiling and walls were opaqued, or polarized, to an unrelieved, dull metallic gray.

Leighton reviewed the tape. He had seen it five times, and each time he imagined he had found something new. He played it once again, this time without sound. Broken-finger's image appeared to float beside John Stranger's in the center of Leighton's executive office. Leighton sat behind an ancient oak desk with its antique fittings and appurtenances, which even included a leather-clad, green blotter and a gold pen and pencil set. He used the pen and pencil; it was one of his few eccentricities.

The old man knew something, but what? Leighton asked himself. Broken-finger had been vague, and that bullshit about John's father hadn't fooled the spotters for a moment. They knew John's history well. That's what he paid them for.

He wondered about a leak. Could the old man have picked up on something? If so, what, and how much? Leighton watched Broken-finger's jaw move up and down on the screen. Just an old man? Maybe. Dangerous? Maybe. He stopped the tape.

In the darkness he pressed a button on the inside well of the desk with his knee.

"Who's on staff at the commissary down there?" he asked.

"Harry Stanton's the front, sir. The red team's underground."

"Send Stanton to Spain. Shift the red team to Utah and bring in a skeleton team. I don't want to take any chances. Has the science staff been moved?"

"Yessir. And I've made provisions to move the entire—"

"Just follow the emergency directive you've been given. Moving the science staff

163

will be sufficient, thank you. I don't want it to look like a goddamn exodus."

"Anything else, Director?"

"Yes, who the fuck gave Stranger a scrambler?"

"An engineer named Taylor Westlake. It didn't work, of course."

"Eliminate him. Make it an accident. And the old man, Broken-finger. . . ."

"You want the same number for him?"

Leighton gazed through the transparent walls at several Trans-United ships floating near a geodesic manufacturing station. Above the geodesic and behind the junk of a jerry-rigged freebooter colony, the mirrored solar collectors hung like the wings of some fantastic rectangular bird. Leighton looked downward, relaxing as he did when he was making a decision. He had the entire room on transparency. It was as if he and his desk were weightless, suspended in space. Below him was the Earth; its hazed horizon looked like it was made of rainbows, as if it were the edge of a fragile soap bubble.

"No, I guess not," he said. "Not yet. He may be useful."

*

John got a break, a small one to be sure, but a break nonetheless. Of the three new people Elliot had assigned to him, one of them happened to be Shawn Rhodes. She was a weapons expert and had worked with watchdogs and flashers. Her experience would at least offset the other new floaters, who would only be in the way no matter how good they were. It was always difficult working with new people. Over the years his crew had grown very close. They had been through the barrel together. It didn't hurt that they were all of Indian extraction, mostly full-bloods, even though they came from different tribes and had different perceptions about the old ways.

As they approached sector omega-ten, John sat suited-up in the cargo area of the transport and talked with Shawn. The cargo area was surrounded by walls of huge boxes. Each gray metal rectangle was numbered. Shorthair said he felt like he was in a post office lobby. Sam Woquini thought they looked more like caskets.

The members of his crew either tied themselves down to the hold-tights as John did or drifted from wall to wall. They were all listening to what Shawn had to say. She spoke quietly. Her voice sounded surprisingly low for such a small woman: she was barely five foot. She was fine-featured: red hair, freckles, and a thin, firm mouth, but her eyes were as hard and penetrating as a duty soldier's.

"This sector has twelve watchdogs, ten of which we own. Basically this is a Trans-United sector, as much as any sector can belong to anybody. One of the other watchdogs belongs to Macro Tech, and the other belongs to the Swiss."

Someone guffawed. Switzerland had been completely overrun after the last fire war. Their underground bases and shelters caved in like mines during the first detonations. The country had been looted as badly as Johannesburg. The Swiss had never regained any power. The banking industry was already settled in the Bahamas, where it was provided with safe haven by unanimous decree of the World Court of Governments and other Polities. Even Continental Cooperative had more satellites than the Swiss, and they were almost entirely a land operation.

"Besides the watchdogs, there are six flashers, two furnaces, and ninety-two remoras, of which we control seventy-three. Like I said, this is a Trans-United area. Something to be thankful for."

John took little comfort in that. Remoras were killers, no matter whom they belonged to. They were programmed to protect and destroy. The small satellites hovered around the watchdogs, blasting anything that got too close. In theory, they wouldn't bother his crew as long as they stayed in the cleared sector. Ray had programmed the defensive satellites to recognize John's crew as *friend*. It wasn't much, but it was something: most space weaponry nowadays was hard wired to accept only limited external programming. The owners of the other remoras and watchdogs had been informed that John's crew was on a routine, *peaceful*, maintenance mission. Supposedly, they had already programmed their satellites accordingly. Supposedly. There was always the possibility that something could go wrong, either accidentally or intentionally, and it was an even chance that someone had snatched the watchdog. Fire wars had started over less. Mexico City had been cluster bombed over a poaching claim ten years ago. In a hundred years or so it might cool off enough to rebuild.

Compared to the watchdogs and remoras, the furnaces were safe. They were just processing plants. The flashers—microwave relay stations—were a problem only if you walked into one of their invisible beams. Yet both furnaces and flashers were potential weapons. Tectonics had lost a crew to an accidental blow-off of a furnace that no one believed was an accident. If someone who knew the command sequence reprogrammed the flasher to turn a quarter of a degree, it could fry a crew or blast a city. Both of these things had happened in the past.

"There's no way we can tell exactly what's wrong until we actually go inside," Shawn continued. "It's probably just a malfunction in the guidance system, which is why they've grabbed you for the job, John.

On the other hand, if it's a snatch, you'll be needing my help."

"If it's a snatch, we'll need more than help," Shorthair said, as he defaced one of the numbered wall caskets with a beam marker. He was drawing little yellow flowers on the metal. He always drew those flowers on every fitting beam and column he bolted together. He never changed the design. "Divine guidance wouldn't be a bad idea."

"Thanks for the encouragement, Shorthair," John said. "I'm always open to constructive suggestions."

The voice of the transport's pilot crackled, "Five minutes to omega-ten, Mr. Stranger."

"Be right up," John said.

John and Shawn floated up the narrow passageway to the control room as the rest of the crew made a last check on their gear. From the bubble in the control room, omega-ten looked, at first glance, to be total blackness broken only by the Earth below them. But John's trained eyes immediately picked up half a dozen remoras—small, hardly visible points of reflected light that were like the eyes of predators in some especially dark jungle night. The remoras were where they were supposed to be. Good. Now if they would only stay there.

The ship moved slowly through omega-ten, following the path Ray Murphy had worked out. As they passed a Swiss watchdog, even John smiled. It was hardly bigger than a council lodge, and the wings of its solar panels needed repair. John could sympathize with the Swiss; his own people had faced hard times for hundreds of years. He hoped the Swiss would pull through.

When the Macro Tech furnace passed in and out of view, John knew they were almost at their destination. The watchdog had already appeared on the pilot's monitor, but John stared out the bubble to see it with his own eyes. At first he could only see scattered specks of light, but then the watchdog came into view. It was a huge sphere. Dull metal. But there was something else there, too. Something deadly.

"Get me Ray on the line," John told the pilot, glancing at Shawn. She had seen it too.

"Murphy here, Stranger."

"What the hell's happening?" John snapped. "There are too fucking many remoras hanging around this watchdog. They can't all be ours."

"They're not," said Ray. "Macro just sent three in there and they've got two more on the way. I don't know why. Nobody tells me anything."

"I'm scrubbing this mission," John said. "Suicide isn't in my nature."

"Can't," Ray said. "Something big's going on with the brass. I tried to pull the plug for you, but Leighton himself told me to keep you out there. Elliot's hanging right over my shoulder to make sure I keep you in line. He's here now."

"Well, fuck Elliot, and fuck Leighton, too. Macro could blast my crew any time it wanted to. I'm not going to sacrifice my people just to keep Trans-United happy."

Shawn gave him a sideways glance. No one stood up to Leighton that way.

"Stranger, you turn back now, and I'll have you and your whole goddamn crew breathing vacuum," Elliot said. "If Leighton wants it, it's big. And he's going to get it. You'd have to take the controls away from your pilot, because he's not going to help you. Isn't that right, Fred?"

The pilot nodded nervously; he didn't look over at John.

"Something else Director Leighton wanted you to know before you kicked out," Elliot continued. "This is a perimeter defense watchdog."

"I know that," John said.

"Well, what you don't know is that if Macro snatched it, the chances are that your home reservation might have been turned into a prime target area."

John felt a chill fan down his back. "Why? There's nothing worth blowing up. It's just fucking desert is all."

"Politics. Maybe Macro just doesn't like Indians. I don't know anything except what Leighton told me to tell you."

John's sharp-featured face was a mask hiding the rekindled hatred he felt for everyone and everything around him, for the very stupidity and venality that had taken all of them this far from the Earth. Yet threaded through the raw hatred was a profound sadness, not only for his crew and the people on his tiny reservation, but for the wasicun, too. They were all caught . . . trapped. He had often had feelings like this in the sweat lodge. The same mixture of hatred and sadness . . . and that was also a kind of love. Hatred wasn't enough to vanquish an enemy.

"I'll get my crew," John said to the pilot. "Take us in."

*

They hovered about fifty meters from the watchdog on a flat, open utility sled launched from the transporter. Remoras the size of a man surrounded them, but kept their distance. The massive watchdog loomed ahead. Small portals pockmarked its side: lasers, a last line of defense in case the remoras failed. The cluster-bomb assembly itself was larger than a house and held not only the multiple warheads, but thousands of scatter-dummies—decoys to fool anyone who tried to intercept the bomb. Directional antennae sprouted all over the watchdog's surface. They would have to be manually aligned after he finished his part of the job. It was a long and tedious process, but others would do that.

His job was simple. Go inside the death machine and fix it.

The plan was to replace the control board for the guidance system and check all the patch lines. If it was a simple malfunction, they should be able to track it down from there. If it had been snatched, however, the whole system would probably be booby-trapped. He'd either get around that or he wouldn't. It was that simple.

Shawn would go in with him.

"Sam, I want you to stay at the sled's controls," John said. "If anything happens, get the crew back to the transport immediately."

"Yes, Mr. Bellman," he said, chuckling, his voice sarcastic. He was joking, making fun of the near-legendary stupidity of most bellmen. After a pause, he said, "This job won't be nothin', you'll see. Sleeptime."

"Well, *you'd* better sleep with your eyes open," John said.

"I always do." The humor had disappeared from Sam's voice, replaced by calmness. Very little bothered him.

"Are you ready?" Shawn asked. John nodded. She drifted off the sled, and with a small burst of nitrogen from his thruster pack, he followed. He half expected a laser to slice through him at any second.

The watchdog looked much larger up

close, and even more deadly. Its antennae twitched and turned, tracking them, along with everything else that moved in this sector. It was like a faceless medusa floating above the Earth.

John and Shawn floated like divers in an ebon ocean to the only entrance into the satellite, a heavy port ringed with lasers and hold-tights. Passing into the dark side of the watchdog, John felt a brush of fear sweep past him like the shadow of a vulture. He clipped his tether to a hold-tight and tried to ignore the laser staring him in the face.

Shawn surprised John by drawing her hand back and forth across her throat; it was a universal signal in space. She wanted him to turn off his intercom so they could speak in private. He nodded and flicked the switch with his tongue. She pressed up against him. From the transport it would look as if they were working on the complicated entrance lock. She touched her helmet to his.

"There's something you should know," she said. Her voice, carrying through the metal and plastic of her helmet, was tinny and distant. "Elliot and Leighton are bullshitting you. This is a worst-possible-case sentry. There must be something down there on Earth that Trans-United wants to hide. If the shit ever hits the fan, this is the sentry that's supposed to take care of the

173

evidence. And if I know about it, you can bet your ass that Macro knows it too."

"Thanks," John said. He understood, but that didn't make it any easier. What it meant was that if Trans-United lost a violent corporate takeover, they would burn their bridges behind them, leaving worthless land and hiding their secrets forever. His homeland was, for reasons he did not understand, one of the bridges to be burned. Literally.

And then he remembered that Leonard Broken-finger had said something about a village of frozen faces. Could that have something to do with all of this?

"We'd better move," John said.

When they switched their intercoms back on, Elliot was yelling. "Why were communications cut?"

"Can it, Elliot," John said. "We had a short, got it fixed. We can either get this job done or sit here and listen to you bitch. Which is it?"

He grumbled, then shut up.

"There, I've got it, John," Shawn said, swinging the entry port open. Feet first, she pulled herself into the small opening. John followed. They both turned on their chest and helmet lamps, which cast an intense, almost pure white light.

There was more room inside than John had expected, but he could almost feel the mass of the cluster bombs around him. The interior of the sentry was starkly functional, full of machinery and complicated, multicolored circuitry. They were surrounded by a metal grid-work which kept them from bumping into anything they shouldn't. The grid was hinged in various places to provide access to the equipment behind it.

Shawn bent over the master control board and studied it intently. John floated behind her, watching over her shoulder.

"As nearly as I can tell, these seals are intact," she said. "They could be phonies, but I don't think so. If this egg's been snatched, it doesn't look like it was done from here. Still, could be a program snatch. . . ."

John didn't need to be told that. He felt wired, as if he was seeing everything with tunnel vision. Broken-finger had once told him when he was a child that it was the gift of danger. John turned and swung open a section of the grid-work. The attitude thruster control system seemed like a logical place to start looking for the problem. He unhooked the probe from his work belt and scrolled down to the proper section of the trouble-shooting pad on his left wrist. Then, while Shawn worked on the board, he examined the coiled, wiry guts of the thruster controls. It wasn't hard work, but it was tedious. There were nearly fifty checkpoints to be reached in this section alone. He had to be painstakingly accurate, and there was no guarantee that the problem was in the thrusters. Carefully, he pushed a knot of wires to one side as he pressed his probe past them to the next checkpoint. The readout was good to six decimal places. He pulled out the probe, arranged the wires as they had been, and moved on.

Then Shawn changed position. After a moment she said, "Sonova*bitch*!" There was a sharp intake of breath in John's intercom. He turned and saw her sprawled against the grid-work on the other side of the room. He could see a tiny hole in her suit below her chest light. Her face plate was frosted over.

John pushed himself off the wall toward her and slapped a quick-seal over the hole. But she twisted as he applied the seal, and John saw her back. It was too late. Between her shoulder blades was a jagged hole, an exit wound, that was larger than his fist. Her suit was shredded, and the wound was a mass of flesh and shattered bone. A pink mist was pouring out of it. Dead, damn it. Booby-trapped.

Then Anna screamed.

He pushed himself toward the exit.

"Remoras!" shouted Red Feather.

John reached the port just as the first remora hit the sled. There was a soundless explosion, a blossom of flame that shattered the sled, spilling debris and his friends in all directions. Another scream: Red Feather gone.

*Red Feather is cold on his heart. There is danger for your people.*

Ray's voice came in loud, overriding everyone else's. It was ragged with panic. "Stranger, it's a snatch. The damn thing's been triggered. Code Blue."

John froze, and the spectacle of death hung before his eyes. His crew was scattered, injured; some were dying or dead. And more would die when the sentry activated. In a few minutes his homeland would become a hole in the desert.

He pushed himself back inside the sentry.

*He fears the fire from the sky. It brings death to his descendants and his people, and somehow your hand is on the fire.*

Code Blue. A forty-five second countdown. It was out of Ray's hands.

John propelled himself to the master control board, gently elbowing Shawn's corpse out of the way. He focused himself, gathered his strength, replaced his panic with a drifting calmness. He thought of the thunder beings, the eagles without form, and he heard the thunder. He took comfort in the familiar sound as he surveyed the board in front of him. Although he had worked on a mock-up of a similar board, it had been over a year ago. He tried to remember.

And it came back to him.

First he looked for a fail-safe, but couldn't find one on this board. Damn, there was no way he could stop the countdown now.

*You will have to make a decision and it will be painful. Death will be all around you like steam in the sweat lodge.*

Shawn had placed a meter and a recoder over the patch points and had slip-jacked them into the circuitry. Its tiny screen blinked and glowed red, indicating that the original hard-wired program had been snatched. The patch points told him something. Beside the primary target there were five backups. But it didn't tell him where they were.

For an instant he floated there, imagining the innocent lives below. He pressed two opposing keys on the meter. It beeped when it found a patch-point coordinate, which appeared in the readout. He had found the newly programmed secondary target. It wasn't the reservation. He could just delete the entire program snatch, but what if Shawn had been right and the reservation was one of the hard-wired Trans-United targets? Then he *would* be the instrument of destruction.

He found the third backup target. That wasn't it either.

Then he found the primary target. It was the reservation and it was part of the jerry-rigged overlay. Leighton had been right. His homeland would be dust in a few minutes.

There was no time to waste. He deleted the snatched program and prayed that the recoder would shunt the bombs to the original hard-wired targets. But what if Shawn had been right, after all? The reservation might still be one of the hard-wired targets.

It was too late.

The sentry rocked violently as the cluster bombs were launched. They were committed now; a fire storm worse than Dresden was headed toward Earth.

Then everything exploded in a burst of blinding white light.

The remoras, guided by unknown hands, were closing in on the sentry and blasting it.

John cartwheeled through space. The sentry had split into several large chunks surrounded by thousands of smaller pieces of debris. Everything tumbled away from the explosion.

The Earth and sun spun vertiginously around him, as if in a dream of falling. The remoras were going crazy. Like a feeding frenzy among sharks, they were shooting at everything that moved. John heard the thunder loud in his ears and felt something cold brush past him—the thunder beings.

His crew was going to die unless he did something.

Using short bursts from the small spot

welder he carried strapped to his left leg, he stopped his somersaulting flight and headed back toward the others. His path was erratic, as he evaded the attacking remoras. He moved without conscious thought, relying on some hidden instinct to second-guess the deadly satellites.

He had the strong intuition that Brokenfinger was somehow watching him . . . guiding him.

The transporter and its crew had fled from the sector; the sled was demolished, his crew scattered. He didn't dare use any radio frequency, lest a remora home in on it.

He found Sam, and they went about the slow and dangerous task of gathering up the rest of the crew. Five were missing, five friends, five brothers and sisters. Anna chased down an oxygen tank from the destroyed sled. They linked themselves together in a long chain, and John used the tank to propel them in a snakelike dance away from the remoras. Omega-ten was a complex sector in the best of times, but now it was a churning nightmare. John held a sharp-edged picture of it in his mind as he threaded the deadly maze. Their progress was slow.

*Your father sees one more thing in his fever. He sees you leading your people.*

It was a long time before they were picked up.

Leighton sat at his desk and leafed through the confidential report of the sentry incident; the flimsy was as thin and light as tissue. This had been a tight one, and there was more to it than appeared in the report. Much more.

One thing was certain. A two-hundred-square-mile area southeast of White Sands was gone, vaporized. It was Macro property, and they had, as Leighton had predicted, made only a minor protest. They claimed thirty lives lost, but his contacts had put the final figure at five hundred and thirty-seven. Fifty-two employees and four hundred and eighty-five sleepers. Macro was keeping quiet because of the sleepers. Deep sleep research was forbidden by international law. Macro claimed it was a microwave receiving station, but it had been a research installation. No matter. Now it was dust.

Ever since the radio signal that came to be known as the Rosetta Triptych was received from the triple-sun system 36 Ophiuchi, Trans-United and Macro had been involved in developing deep sleep. Each corporation wanted to make the first contact with a technologically superior alien race. Using the Cristal-Williston Fusion Drive, which had been successfully tested, and deep sleep, contact could be made in less than a hundred years. Not so much time in corporate terms, for corporations, unlike nation-states, were used to long-range planning.

Then last year a minor-ranking scientist working for Trans-United discovered a way to get around the neural synapse problem. One of Macro's spies got hold of the information and an undeclared corporate war began. But after a failed Trans-United deep-sleep experiment was leaked into the news-net, the public outcry was immediate and strong. As luck would have it, one of Macro's mass graves of sleepers was also discovered by a reporter for one of the most popular sleazy yellow shows. And that immediately became hot news. Within weeks the World Court had outlawed all deep-sleep experimentation. After that, the corporations purged the rank and file of their security sections and simply moved their operations to other underground sites. Eventually the outcry died down.

The sentry ploy had been a gamble, but a carefully planned gamble. Any investigation would show that Trans-United's own property and personnel had been in danger, and that would clear the company of any suspicion. It would look like a program snatch. Leighton had banked on John Stranger's overwhelming tribal loyalty and ability to make instant decisions to pull it off. And it had worked. There would be no serious investigation.

Leighton shifted in his chair and depolarized the room. As the room lights were lowered, a thousand stars bathed the stark room in a wan, milky haze. Leighton felt like an Olympian god gazing out from the heavens. He tapped his fingers on his polished desk top and tried to decide what would be the best use of the corporate asset known as John Stranger.

*

Held in place by restraint webbing that surrounded him like a loosely fitting cocoon, John floated in the recovery room. Med-patches covered his arms and chest, delivering carefully measured doses of medications. Above him a monitor blinked and clicked softly with reassuring regularity. He drifted with his eyes closed and his mind troubled.

John could not stop dwelling on what he might have done differently in those last few seconds inside the sentry. He had traded the lives of strangers for the lives of his family and friends. A feeling of helpless remorse filled him as he wondered about the people he had caused to die ... the people he had killed.

Finally he fell asleep, slowly falling through the suffocating layers of guilt and exhaustion to a spirit world cobbled out of fever dreams. He saw Broken-finger. It was afternoon. The sky was clear. There was

183

barely any wind, and the only sound was the buzzings of flies.

Broken-finger looked into John.

*You must make your decision and then not look back. You must not punish yourself for the thing you have done.*

The old man spread his arms, and they turned into wings. His face melted into the terrible mask of the thunder beings. The thunder being rose into the air, its great wings making the sound of a bellows pumping, and John looked into the face of death.

And saw himself.

He was the thunder being.

Taking life.

Giving life.

Turning and crying in his sleep.

# THE TOR DOUBLES

Two complete short science fiction novels in one volume!

# THE BEST IN SCIENCE FICTION

# BESTSELLING BOOKS FROM TOR

# PHILIP JOSÉ FARMER